The Last Adventure of Garrius Arilius

ALSO BY KARL EL-KOURA

Father John VS the Zombies

Ooter's Place and Other Stories of Fear, Faith, and Love

The Lost Stories: A Series of Cosmic Adventures

KARL EL-KOURA

The Last Adventure of Garrius Arilius

Publication History

A modified version of Part One of this book was published as "The Pursuit of Garrius Arilius" in Issue 5, Volume 2 (February 2004) of *Penumbric Speculative Fiction Magazine*.

For more information, visit:
www.ootersplace.com/LastAdventure

To George

Contents

Part One
Pursuit

I'M looking for Garrius Arilius," the young man said, standing awkwardly by Garrius's table. "I was told you'd know where I can find him."

Garrius continued staring at the couple at the far corner of the tavern. The woman—a girl, really—looked distinctly uncomfortable and her male companion didn't look like he'd had an honorable intention in his entire life.

The man by Garrius's table forced a cough. "If you'll just tell me where to find him," he said, speaking a little more forcefully this time. "I can pay you very well."

Garrius tore his gaze away from the couple and fixed it on the young man. *If he was twenty years old*, Garrius thought, *it hadn't happened more than a year ago.* He had brown hair that fell to his shoulders and a small brown beard that circled his mouth. A gold-laced green tunic draped the length of his body and probably cost as much as most people earned in a year.

"Garrius owe you money?"

"Oh, no. It's nothing like that."

"Good. You would've never seen it."

The young man's eyebrows drew together.

"Garrius is dead," Garrius said. "Died last night,

right here in this tavern. A knife-fight with a big guy. Ten feet if he was an inch."

The perplexed look on the young man's face gave way to one of utter disappointment. "It can't be," he said. "I've come so far to find him."

Garrius smiled sympathetically, then let his gaze return to the couple. Their seats were empty.

In a flash, he leapt from the table, his seat toppling over by the force of his departure, and was out the door.

Three streets connected to the tavern, each one as dark as the next. He peered into the darkness and listened, but he couldn't see or hear anything to help him pick a direction.

How had he let them slip away?

With a frustrated grunt he tore down the middle street, stopping only when he saw or thought he saw a shadowy figure hunched over in a dark corner, or when he heard something that could be a muffled scream. At a certain point, pushing away the feelings of frustration, he decided to double back and try the left-hand street, then the right-hand street after that, where he finally heard what he'd been listening for. He followed the sound of the whimpering and found the young girl in an alley so dark he almost couldn't make her out from the shadows cast by the surrounding buildings.

Her clothes were torn and blood gushed from a deep cut along the right side of her face. She stared at him with eyes that didn't see, and was whispering to herself the words of a lullaby he didn't recognize.

Garrius picked her up—did she feel extremely light or was that his imagination?—and placed her against the wall of one of the buildings. She didn't recoil from his touch; she hardly seemed aware that she was being moved at all.

Whispering a prayer, he pressed his hands against her belly. It was unmistakable: there was a growing emptiness inside. He swallowed hard, then pulled out his dagger, whispered, "May Thephis have mercy on your soul," and slit her throat.

He wiped the dagger on his leg with more force than was strictly necessary, then replaced it in its sheath. From the corner of his eye, he caught a glimpse of a figure rounding the corner that led back to the street; a few seconds later, he caught the escaping figure itself and pinned it against the stone wall in a beam of moonlight.

"You killed her," the young man from the tavern stammered, his eyes wide, his forehead sweaty, his breathing labored and raspy. "I saw you."

"I should kill you, too," Garrius said, not attempting to mask the contempt in his voice. "It's your fault this happened." He let the man go and and started to move away.

"*You're* Garrius Arilius, aren't you?" the young man said, following him. "You're Garrius Arilius." The sentence managed to be a statement, a question and an accusation all at once. "But you're supposed to be this great hero—and you're nothing but a damned murderer! And a liar!"

Garrius kept moving.

Dirt and stones hit his back as he heard the young man whisper, "*Vox ex pox!*"

Garrius came to a stop, turned around slowly. "What did you say?"

The young man stared at him defiantly. "You'll find out soon enough, unless you explain what happened!"

Garrius rolled his eyes. "You'd be smart to leave me alone," he said, walking away again.

"Aren't you afraid I'll go to the Guard?" the young man called out.

Garrius didn't slow his pace or look back, but he knew that the young man wasn't following him any longer.

Back at the tavern, Garrius asked the owner if she had any vacant rooms.

"Just the one room to let is all I've got," she said, flashing a friendly, toothless grin. "But it's yours if you want it."

They settled on a price and Garrius paid her, giving the old lady a little extra to make sure no one bothered him while he slept. He followed her outside and around the back to a wooden door that looked like it might come loose if someone were foolhardy enough to move it. But the old lady swung it open without hesitation and slipped inside. She reemerged a few moments later, pushing in front of her a teenaged boy who'd obviously been roused from sleep and not yet given a chance to get fully dressed.

"It's all yours," she said, winking. "Nighty night."

"What about him?"

"Never mind the boy," the old lady said, slapping him across the back of the head to make him get out of the way. "He's had enough sleep, he has."

The room was small and dirty, the furnishings consisting entirely of a bed with a wooden frame that had begun to fall apart and rot away. Touching the ceiling above the bed was a window that looked into the tavern and allowed the light from there to enter the room. Sheets that had once been white covered the bed; Garrius pulled them off and tossed them into a corner.

He hung his sword on the bedpost, undressed, then sunk gratefully into the bed.

The nightmares began as soon as he closed his eyes.

H E kept his eyes closed when he awoke. Someone was in the room with him. Garrius listened for a moment, then turned over, jumped out of bed, and grabbed and unsheathed his sword.

The young man from the night before stood near the door. "I'm not here to harm you," he said nervously, his gaze fixed on the end of the long sword. "I'm not armed."

"What do you want?" Garrius said, slipping the sword back into its sheath. "How did you get in here? Damn that old woman."

"Don't worry," the young man said. "She didn't sell you cheaply."

Garrius began to dress.

"I'm giving you a chance to explain about last night," the young man said. "And I want to know what you did with the body."

Garrius finished dressing.

He strapped the sword's scabbard to his back and pushed past the young man and out the door. It was very early in the morning, when the night's chill had not yet been chased away by the rising sun, but he found the slight breeze of cool air refreshing. The sky was cloudless and blue.

Drawing in a deep breath, he decided to drop into the tavern for a quick drink before continuing to Quisin. He told himself it would give him a chance to glare at the money-soft old lady, but a part of him wondered if his nerves were finally failing him and he was trying to delay his encounter with the Old Witch.

Two guardsmen pointed their lances at his nose as he turned the corner. He didn't need to look over his shoulder to know that two more had come up behind him, their lances pointed at the back of his head.

"Can I help you gentlemen?" Garrius said, seemingly oblivious to the men behind him.

The guard on the left spoke up first. "You have been accused of murder. You will accompany us to the Court of Justice and stand trial."

Stand trial on nothing but an accusation? Garrius thought. *How much money has that kid been spreading around?*

"That's fine," he said. "I've been dying to see the Court of Justice, actually."

Suddenly a pained expression seized Garrius's face and he looked down at his feet; as the guardsmen's gazes followed his, he turned on his heels, yanked the two lances out of the hands of the men behind him, then swung them towards the other guardsmen's heads. The lances made contact with a resounding, painful *crack* that made him sorry he'd used quite so much force. Both men dropped to the ground, their hands clutching their heads, as Garrius ducked, spun around, and knocked out the legs from underneath the remaining two men.

He could forget about that drink, he knew.

At the stables he retrieved Asher, then walked him to the city gates as quickly as he could manage without arousing suspicion. He made it past the gate guard and out the gates and was already atop his horse and riding when he heard the alarm go up.

G ARRIUS leapt off Asher at a distance from the river,

and made him wait there, which Asher was only too happy to do; for some reason Garrius had never uncovered, large bodies of water unnerved Asher.

He'd been riding for three days, resting himself and Asher only during the darkest hours of the night before starting up again. He now felt confident that he'd lost anyone who might have given chase from the city. Either way, though, he was tired and thirsty, his horse was tired and thirsty, and this forest seemed a good place to regain their strength.

At the edge of the river, he filled up his canteen and gulped down the clean and deliciously cold water. He made several trips from the river to Asher, filling up the small canteen half a dozen times before the horse had finally satisfied his thirst.

A large rock overgrown with moss was positioned a short distance from the river on a soft-looking patch of grass. He leaned his sword and overcoat against one side of the rock, and his back against another. The ground around him was sprinkled with some twigs and fallen leaves and a few insects scurrying about and burrowing in the ground. A brown snake tried to slither past him, but Garrius had no sooner noticed it than plunged his dagger through its head. He picked up its dead body with the blade of the dagger and flung it far away.

Finally he allowed his heavy head to drop against the cushion of the moss on the rock, and he slowly fell asleep. Again he dreamt of Priscilla; dreamt of her body being eaten alive from the inside out; dreamt of her pleading, begging, crying; dreamt of himself, horrified and watching helplessly as the dying body he cradled in his arms slowly disappeared, piece by piece.

When he awoke, he couldn't open his eyes. Something was covering his face...the moss. Somehow the moss had enveloped his head while he slept. *Magic*, he thought. *Powerful magic.*

He tried to free himself, but the more he struggled, the tighter the moss gripped his face. He tried reaching for his sword, but the moss had grown to overtake his shoulders and he was only able to bend his arms at the elbows. He did manage to get hold of the dagger strapped to his thigh, but it proved ineffective against the thick moss, which continued its slow expansion down his body.

The moss was well past his hips when he first heard the horses. Their hoofs beating against the ground made a sound like thunder. He had been lying perfectly still, not wanting to force the moss into gripping him more tightly, trying to think of a way out when he felt the ground shake and heard the thunderous hoof beats.

Trying to move as little as possible, he began to yell for help. As soon as he opened his mouth and started screaming, he felt the moss's advance come to a sudden halt. He raised his voice again, and felt the moss retreat from his upper right leg—it moved a lot quicker when retreating than the snail's crawl it used to advance. He raised his voice even louder, yelling blood-curdling battle cries. The moss pulled away even faster.

He hardly paused for breath, elated that he had finally found an escape out of this enclosing prison. He yelled until his shoulders were free, at which point he gave his lungs and throat a break and reached for his sword. If *it* could not cut through the moss, he thought, nothing made by human hands or otherwise ever could.

His sword was not where he had left it. And now that he wasn't yelling, he heard from all around him the sound of neighing and the clinking of jewels and armor as the horses kicked up their feet. He hoped the moss still enveloping his head was amplifying the sound from the horses; otherwise, he was about to face a small army... exhausted and without his sword.

He heard something else then, the voice of the young man from the tavern. The moss responded by falling away from Garrius immediately, like a reprimanded child pulling back its hands from something it shouldn't have touched. Garrius blinked to clear his eyes, then saw, behind the young man, a small army indeed. All sorts of weapons were pointed at him—lances, swords, arrows ready to fly from their bows.

"I don't think you're a murderer," the young man said, kneeling beside Garrius and whispering. "These men are in my employ. Tell me you didn't murder her and I'll dismiss them."

"If I had not killed her," Garrius said, whispering back, "you would've seen something much worse than a man slitting a girl's throat."

There was silence between them for a short while. Then the young man stood up and held out his hand to Garrius, who took it and pulled himself up.

"Return his sword," the young man said, without looking behind him. A horseman galloped forward and handed the sword to Garrius.

To that horseman, the young man tossed a light brown pouch tied with purple lace. "You and your men are free to go," he said. "I thank you for your service."

The horseman bowed his head, then yelled out a command and, turning his horse, rode out of the forest with his men following. The young man tightly gripped the reins of his horse, who neighed and looked at the retreating horses wistfully.

"You are too trusting, friend," Garrius said. "One day you may trust the wrong person."

"But not today," the young man said, smiling. "My name is Milos."

Garrius took the offered hand and said, "Garrius Arilius."

"I know," Milos said. He shook his head but the smile hadn't dropped from his face; it seemed to Garrius it had rather expanded triumphantly.

Garrius strapped his sword to his back and returned to Asher.

"I ride to Quisin," Garrius said. "It is a journey of two more days. Ride with me and I will try to explain about the girl as best I can."

WHATEVER else he may be, the young man was a good listener. They rode their horses at a trot, Garrius talking and Milos interrupting only to ask a question or two for clarification.

"There is a creature," Garrius began, "who has the ability to turn into the shape of any man it wishes. Or perhaps it is able to possess men's bodies, I don't know. There is a lot about this matter I don't know.

"However it acquires a human body, this creature seduces women and lies with them, leaving them full of silk-thin silvery snakes that crawl through the rest of their bodies and begin to eat their way out. When the snakes are finished, there is nothing left of the woman's body. No bones, no blood, no flesh. No sign at all that she ever lived or died."

"And the woman you killed was filled with these snakes?" Milos said. "So that is why we found no trace of her body! Even the blood you had spilled from her throat was gone!"

"The snakes are ravenous. They leave nothing behind."

"But we have to warn the others! We have to go back!"

"When they are finished devouring their prey, the snakes vanish. They are magical creatures conjured for a single purpose."

"Who conjured them?"

"That is why I go to Quisin. There is a seer there who may be able to answer my questions."

"I knew you weren't a murderer," Milos said thoughtfully. "But couldn't a healer or a priest have done something for her?"

Garrius didn't answer right away. When he did, his voice was soft enough that Milos rode his horse closer to Garrius to hear him. "I once watched someone get eaten alive by the snakes," he said. "It was quick...not quick enough...but it was over within minutes."

If Milos noticed the tears that had formed in Garrius's eyes, he pretended that he didn't. "She was close to you?"

"She was my wife."

"I'm sorry," Milos said. Then, as he reached the obvious conclusion, he began to say, "She was un—" but quickly cut himself off.

Garrius turned his head to look at the young man, who was blushing and staring at the road ahead.

"I wasn't a good husband to her," Garrius said. "At first, maybe, but not towards the end." He took a deep breath. "She was only answering in kind."

There was a silence between them even longer than the first. The sun blazed in the sky; the day had grown warmer, and now that they had left the forest and the protective cover the trees provided, they were relieved only by a merciful wind of cool air.

"I'm very sorry about your wife," Milos said finally.

Garrius pulled out his canteen and took a few sips. "You wanted something from me," he said. "At the tavern."

"Yes, and I'm doing it."

"Excuse me?"

"Adventuring with Garrius Arilius! Seeing the world! Righting wrongs! Together we ride to Quisin"— Milos pronounced it incorrectly—"to find a way to rid the world of this evil plague of snakes." He sat taller on his horse. "This is what it's about," he said, seeming to speak mostly to himself. "I've been cooped up under my father's protective wings all my life, my entire world consisting of a castle and some acres of palace grounds. But this—this is it."

"Ah, so it's Prince Milos, then?" Garrius said with feigned respect.

"Please no," Milos said. "I walked away from all that."

"Not all of it, I see," Garrius said, pointing with his chin at the young man's tunic. "So why did you choose me?"

Milos was blushing, either at the comment or the question. But it seemed to Garrius that Milos blushed at the slightest provocation.

"Do you remember a man named King Baldou?"

"Yes."

"Do you remember his daughter?"

Garrius laughed as the image of the feisty little princess jumped into his mind. "Oh yes, how could I forget? She wanted to come on adventures with me, and raised quite the storm when I refused." He laughed again. "I haven't often felt very intimated in my life, but I certainly did when standing between that little girl and what she wanted."

"Then the years haven't changed her very much," Milos said, smiling.

Garrius turned an inquisitive look on him.

"She is my betrothed. It was all arranged between her father and mine. Both of us—myself and Anya, I mean—were very much against the idea, me because I didn't know if I was ready for marriage, and she for her own reasons. Except that I changed my mind when I saw her."

"But she didn't change her mind?"

Milos shook his head. "She was very nice about it, in her own way. Whatever her father's wishes, she didn't intend to marry anyone she didn't respect. And how could she respect me? I'd lived an easy, sheltered life. She wanted to know if I were a hero or a villain before she married me—but I've never had the chance to prove I'm either one.

"Anyway," he continued, "if she didn't respect me, she couldn't love me. And if she didn't love me, she wouldn't marry me."

"Okay," Garrius said, confused about his own role in the young man's love life. "So you think that hanging around me will make her love you?"

"No, of course not. But I do want her to respect me; the rest will follow if it's meant to. But even more than anything to do with her, I want to respect myself, Garrius. She opened my eyes about the kind of person I am and the kind of life I've lived, and now I can't shut them even if I'd want to." Milos was blushing again. "When I asked her what I should do, she said we should seek out a man named Garrius Arilius. Spend time with him, face what he faced, stand by him in battle, and learn from him about honor and courage."

"We?"

"The plan was to find you together and convince you to let us accompany you. We made the mistake of telling our parents, though. King Baldou refused to let us travel together unless we were married. So I talked her into waiting until I'd proven myself first. But my father refused to let me go at all—he went so far as to imprison me in my own room." Milos flashed a rueful smile. "By now he's discovered I'm no longer there. It's been a long time since a locked door and some guards can stop me from slipping out! I escaped with the money I had in my room...most of which I've spent tracking you down. But look at me now—just this morning I rescued Garrius Arilius from killer moss bent on suffocating him to death!"

"That moss was harmless until you came along," he said, as Milos laughed. Garrius had forced his voice to sound playful, but inwardly he couldn't help but feel a pang of jealousy at Milos's story. Were things ever so simple for him? Had decisions ever seemed so clear-cut? This young man hadn't yet made any fatal mistakes; he hadn't deeply hurt someone he loved, hadn't been deeply hurt himself. His life was ahead of him, and his only concern was winning the love of a beautiful princess, for whom he'd turned his back on the luxuries of palace life.

Garrius tried to push those thoughts away. And yet—his own love was behind him. His failures were many, his wounds deep. There were sights his mind would never let him forget, painful words and visions his heart repeated incessantly to him, late at night when he tried to sleep. What he would give for a fresh start—a chance to see Priscilla again, and be with her, and love her the way he should have the first time around.

He took a deep breath. The path from jealousy to self-pity was a short one, and well-worn. He'd hoped himself above such feelings. But there had been a time when he had thought himself above fear, too.

Congratulations, brave warrior, he told himself, *you were not defeated by armies or sorcerers or ogres, but by yourself. It's the monsters you've grown in your own heart who will defeat you in the end.*

Milos was staring at him. "So you're really not going to ask me about the moss, huh?" he said. "Aren't you curious how I did it?"

Garrius looked away. "I don't much care for magic." In fact, his distaste for magic, if as irrational as Asher's distaste for large bodies of water, was at least as strong.

"That's because you've never seen my kind of magic!" Milos said. "Here, stop your horse for a minute."

Reluctantly, Garrius did so and turned to face the young man.

Milos held up his hands and touched his thumbs. He then brought his index fingers together so that the four fingers formed a triangle. As soon as the index fingers touched, the face of the triangle became solid.

Garrius reached out and tapped the blue face of the triangle with a fingernail. It made a sound like hard metal.

"Not bad," Garrius said, forcing a smile.

"Try your sword against it," Milos said with a dramatic smile, placing the triangle over his heart.

Garrius paused only a moment before pulling out his sword. In that moment, he'd decided he would pierce

Milos's flesh. Only a little, certainly nowhere near deep enough to touch his heart. It was important that the boy learn not to be overconfident about his powers. He hoped the experience might even turn him away from magic altogether. "All right," he said, then thrust his sword at the young man's heart.

The triangle didn't break. The face was as blue as ever; his sword hadn't caused so much as a scratch.

"I'm impressed," Garrius said, trying to mask how impressed he really was.

Milos smiled happily and dropped his hands. "I taught myself how to do that."

"You did?" Garrius said.

"Yes—and making the moss trap you. That was the hex I put on you after you killed that girl. It was supposed to help me locate you, and then hold you in place when I got close. But I didn't realize the moss would be so...aggressive. Sometimes my magic isn't very disciplined."

Garrius didn't respond right away; he tried to keep his face neutral as he looked at Milos. If he'd learned to do all of that by himself, Garrius thought, his aptitude for magic must be very strong. With proper training, he could become a powerful magician, perhaps as powerful or even more powerful than Vladmin had been.

"We better keep going," Garrius said, turning his gaze away from the young man, urging Asher forward, and praying with all of his heart that Milos would never get proper training.

THAT night, unable to sleep, Garrius thought of his brother.

He remembered when they were around nine and seven years old, and Garrius was in the forest near their father's castle, swinging his sword, battling giant trees as if they were giant monsters. Vladmin was watching his older brother, as he almost always did. Around the castle, some of the servants joked that Vladmin was simply Garrius's shadow, and it was supposed that he would cease to exist if Garrius ever did.

"This tyrant has kidnapped a beautiful princess," Garrius said, turning suddenly on a tree and chopping off one of its branches in a swift, ax-like motion. "And this one," he said, turning his attention and sword on the unfortunate tree, "is terrorizing one of father's villages."

"This one owes father money," his brother said, leaping to attack it.

"Where did you get that?" Garrius said.

Instead of answering, his brother shrugged and the sword disappeared.

It was a turning point in their relationship. Vladmin had discovered ground where he could compete with—and beat—Garrius. Garrius didn't like magic and had never developed the talent; Vladmin was so good by the time he was thirteen that he could make himself invisible and hide in the castle, and none of the king's magicians could find him.

When Garrius was sixteen, he could barely stand to be around his brother any longer. Vladmin was cruel with his power; he terrorized the castle's servants by animating their brooms or making doors open and shut, or turning castle furniture into gruesome creatures. Their father was doing nothing about it. Perhaps he was afraid of Vladmin. Or perhaps he had come to rely too much on Vladmin and his powers, because he used his son to spy on his enemies.

Garrius reached his breaking point when he was seventeen. He and Priscilla had gone horseback riding, across green fields and up and down rolling hills. They were unpacking their lunch just inside the entrance to a forest, the trees providing welcome shade from the afternoon sun. There was a garden snake slithering near the white sheet they had laid out on the ground. Garrius and Priscilla noticed it at the same time. Garrius nodded slightly and with a sudden, quick motion, Priscilla reached out and grabbed the snake.

With an audible *pop*, the snake disappeared and a foot or two away from them Vladmin stood, a big smile spread across his face.

"What's for lunch?" he said.

"Less magic and more manners would do you good, Vladmin," Priscilla said.

"You must have respect for other people's privacy," Garrius said.

"Both of you are quick to dole out advice, I see," Vladmin said, still standing in front of them. "And I? To whom shall I give advice? Shall I advise father to forbid your marriage? I have his ear, you know. Shall I advise him to forbid the marriage of his son, Prince of Trydon and heir to its throne, to this—"

Garrius didn't allow him to finish the sentence. He leapt to his feet and knocked Vladmin off of his, almost as if in a single motion.

"I've warned you before," Garrius said. "You don't want to talk about Priscilla like that."

"You choose common riff-raff over royal blood?" Vladmin said, speaking from the ground and through his hand; he held his jaw as if it were broken. "Over family?"

Garrius didn't answer. Vladmin stood up very slowly. Ignoring Garrius, he focused his dark gaze on Priscilla. Although Vladmin had never been kind to Priscilla, there was now a hatred in his eyes that Garrius had never seen there before.

"I forbid you to marry my brother," he said, his voice firm and chilling. "If you value your life, do not marry him."

Garrius left Trydon the next day, taking nothing with him. He and Priscilla journeyed out alone, to build their life together in a quiet village far away.

They never spoke of Vladmin's threat. Even still, and although Priscilla would never have acknowledged it, and maybe never even have admitted it to herself, Garrius saw, much later when Vladmin was killed, that it was as if a heavy burden had been lifted from her shoulders.

IT was perhaps appropriate, Garrius thought, that the Old Witch—if she had another name, Garrius had never heard it—chose to live in Quisin. In his travels he'd seen many cities and villages, but none as miserable as this one. Quisin's buildings consisted of rotten wood held together by rusted nails. Its streets were paved with mud and beggars; in many cases, it was impossible to tell with eyes alone where the mud ended and the beggar began. Homeless children scurried the streets like rats, pick-pocketing any passerby who looked like they might have something worth stealing, taunting and making sport of the rest. Whores advertised themselves openly; some even worked openly, in side alleys or in houses with the curtains left undrawn.

He and Milos walked their horses through the streets, Milos looking both disgusted and fascinated at the same time. He stared at the beggars, perhaps unsure whether they were flesh-and-blood creatures or mud-formed statues. When a toothless whore called out to him, he blushed and shook his head vigorously.

Garrius couldn't help but notice that Milos was breathing through his mouth; small blue circles filled his nostrils. Milos saw him staring. "Do you want me to plug your nose?"

Garrius looked away. "You get used to the smell after a while," he said.

The children kept their distance; upon entering the city, Garrius had unsheathed his sword and begun to swing it distractedly in slow circles, allowing everyone the opportunity to notice how big and sharp it was.

The Old Witch's house was the only one in the city not made entirely of wood. The walls consisted of smoothed-out stones, each the size of a man's torso. The shuttered windows, the large door, and the planks supporting the roof were made from wood that Garrius could tell had been magically treated. Unlike the rest of the city's, this wood would never rot—and it couldn't be cut or broken by the sharpest ax or strongest shoulder.

Garrius handed his sword to Milos and said, "Take care of Asher. I won't be long." *I hope*, he added to himself.

"I'll chance whatever's in there. It can't be worse than standing out here."

You have no idea. He'd started to shake his head, thought of explaining how dangerous the witch could be, thought of telling Milos how many people had gone in but never come out. But he decided it would be better to try a different approach. "I know it's dangerous out here," he said, "but I need you to stay and keep an eye on our horses. Otherwise they'll be gone the second we turn our backs on them."

Milos didn't bother fighting the smile that came to his lips. His grip on Garrius's sword became firmer.

"Hold it menacingly," Garrius said, positioning himself in front of the Old Witch's door. He knocked. The door opened, seemingly of its own volition. When Garrius went through, it snapped shut behind him.

From the walls of the room hung the heads of those who had lost their lives and souls to the Old Witch, gruesome trophies whose flesh was kept from decomposing by her magic. The severed heads, with their unblinking eyes and grisly smiles, covered the walls from floor to ceiling. There was nothing else in the small room; even the Old Witch was missing.

Not knowing what else to do, he found himself succumbing to the morbid compulsion to study the faces on the wall. Some of them belonged to young girls, perhaps not more than eight or nine. Others belonged to old men, with wrinkled skin and sunken eyes. Some were the faces of fierce-looking warriors; many looked like the whores and beggars that littered the streets of Quisin. Garrius found himself full of curiosity about them. What were their stories? What questions did they want answered so badly that they would gamble their lives and their souls? And what had the Old Witch said that caused them to give themselves over to her for eternity?

He was studying one of the faces, a wizened man whose tiny black eyes reminded him of his father's, when the head began speaking.

"Look who it is," it said in a gruff voice. "Didn't I

tell you you'd be back?"

"I didn't come here to play games, old woman."

The man's head shrieked in laughter.

"All right, then," he heard from behind him, in a different voice. A soft voice, a feminine voice, a sing-songy voice that was all too familiar.

Garrius turned and found himself looking at his wife's severed head on the opposite wall. He fell back, a horrified gasp escaping from his mouth.

"You're cheating," he said when he had regained his composure. "Let her spirit rest." His heart wrenched in pain and the feeling of emptiness in his stomach grew even more and threatened to overcome him, but he drew himself up to his full height and returned the head's unblinking stare. "You will play fair, old woman," he said, his voice loud and firm. "My wife's soul is hers, not yours. Let her spirit rest!"

"Over here," spoke another head in a different voice to his right. Garrius instinctively turned to face it. He quickly turned back to look for his wife's head on the wall, and was grateful when he couldn't find it.

"Before I answer your questions," the head, that of a child, said, "do you want to hear something?"

Garrius nodded.

The child's head shrieked in laughter. "The young man who waits outside will have his head impaled upon your sword before this sun has fallen."

Garrius pushed the gruesome image out of his mind immediately. The child's head seemed to want to say more; Garrius nodded for it to go on.

"You will put it there."

Garrius began to shake his head and protest, but stopped himself. "Anything else?"

"When you found your wife, the snakes had already been in her for minutes, feasting on her guts, chewing through her bones, drinking her blood. You cannot imagine the pain she suffered or the terror that gripped her heart."

Again Garrius chased away the mental images conjured by the Old Witch's words. But even before he could nod, the child's head went on, in a voice filled with urgency:

"You couldn't save her, but others will suffer like her. There is a way to save them! There is a way for young Milos outside to live and for the creature to die. Release your soul to me. If you die, the creature dies with you. Quickly, Garrius—before it has a chance to kill again!"

Garrius stared speechless at the severed head.

"It ends now, Garrius," the Old Witch said from behind him. He turned around again; the old woman herself stood in the middle of the room, hunched over a wooden cane whose handle was shaped like a human skull. She wore a black hooded cape that fell to her ankles; the hood of the cape left her face in impenetrable shadow. Her neck was dark-skinned and lined with wrinkles.

She pointed at some of the heads on the walls with her cane. "You thought they were all cowards, didn't you? That they lost their souls to me because they couldn't stand to hear the truth or because their fear got the better of them?

"Well, that's certainly true of some," she continued, her cane sweeping over a few seemingly random faces. "But not of others." Her cane suddenly dropped to point straight at him. "It wouldn't be true of you, Garrius.

"The creature is here in Quisin; you brought it here.

It has already met its next victim. The only way to save her is to sacrifice yourself, right now. Otherwise she dies."

"Answer my questions quickly," Garrius said. "I decide after you answer my questions!"

The old woman let the cane drop to the ground.

"Where did this creature come from?" Garrius said.

"It was conjured."

"Conjured by whom?"

"Who else has the power? Your brother, of course."

Garrius closed his eyes. Of all the possible answers the Old Witch could have given him, this was the worst —Vladmin was still alive. Garrius had left him for dead, buried under the ruins of their father's castle, sapped of the dark magic whose energy had turned him into a power-hungry tyrant. Had Vladmin been regaining his strength all these years? Was this creature the first arrow in his strike against Garrius?

"How do I recognize it?" Garrius asked. "How do I fight it?"

The old woman was silent. After a moment, she said, "The young woman is infected. Her name was Tishna. You waited too long." He heard her sigh.

Garrius jumped forward but resisted the urge to grab the old woman. "Answer my question!" he yelled in her shadowed face. "How do I fight it?"

The old woman took a step back before answering. "The creature is a snake the size of my cane," she said. "It is called Orobo, is invisible to eyes such as yours, and cannot survive outside a human body for very long. Orobo burrows into a victim's head—a male victim, understand?—and wraps itself around his brain. Within seconds, Orobo has complete control. It uses his body's resources to produce offspring. These ravenous little snakes can't travel through the air but they"—the old woman cut herself off mid-sentence and laughed— "but you already know all about that, don't you, my friend?"

Garrius didn't respond.

"Orobo stays with the male host for as long as it can, using his body as a factory to produce more children and to implant them into more victims. When it has depleted the host's resources, Orobo devours what's left of him and moves on to the next male victim."

"How do I kill it?" Garrius said.

"There are two ways. Die and the creature dies with you, by the rules of its magic. You understand? But Orobo will never infect you, only those around you."

Garrius's eyes widened in horror, but again he forced himself to remain silent. How was it that he could still marvel at the depths of Vladmin's cruelty?

"No, your brother has a different end in mind for you," the old woman was saying. "Believe me, Garrius, it would be better for you not to fall into his hands. Give yourself to me and—"

"Tell me the other way," he said, cutting her off.

"The creature has exhausted its present host. It searches for its next male victim. It is moving towards your friend outside."

Garrius's gaze jumped to the door.

The old woman said, "That is the other way. In a few moments, your friend will become infected. Just step outside and drive your sword through his head. Or give yourself to me now and let your friend live."

It seemed to him an impossible situation. He couldn't give himself up, not with Vladmin still alive. He had promised Priscilla that he would stop his brother, an obligation he had thought fulfilled. He would gladly trade his own life to save the lives of others—especially now when his death meant reunion with rather than separation from his wife, Thephis willing—but he couldn't allow himself to die, not until he'd put an end to Vladmin's tyranny. What choice did that leave him, though? Stand by and allow his young friend to become infected? And then what? Plunge a sword through the head of the young, happy man who—

That train of thought came to a sudden stop, a triumphant smile sweeping over his face as the answer appeared to him fully-formed in his mind. He lunged for the door.

It was locked.

He turned and yelled, "Open it!"

She pointed her cane at him once more and said, "The third time will be your last, Garrius. Stay away if you can."

The door came open and Garrius flew through it.

Milos stood by the horses, looking bored.

"What kept you so long?" he said, a slightly annoyed expression on his face.

Garrius tore his sword out of the young man's hand. Staring intensely into Milos's eyes, he said, speaking quickly, "If you value your life, do as I say. Form a shield inside your head to protect your brain."

Garrius grabbed the young man's neck with one hand, and raised his sword with the other, pointing it at Milos's head.

Milos tried to fall back, but Garrius held him tightly in place. The young man's eyes were filled with fear and confusion.

"Do it," Garrius said. "Use your magic to form a shield around your brain."

"I can't," the young man said, in a choked voice. "I don't know—"

"Do it!" Garrius yelled as he saw Milos wince in pain and a small hole appear at the side of his neck.

He threw Milos's body to the ground, gripped his sword with both hands and, pausing only long enough to offer a silent prayer to Thephis, plunged the sword through the young man's skull.

THE creature was dead.

Would the nightmares die with it? Garrius wondered. And if they didn't, would he be able to face and defeat his brother? Against dark magic, the surest defense was a disciplined and focused mind. But Garrius's mind was now a tempest—of doubt, of fear, but mostly of visions and images it took most of his effort to keep at bay.

Again he pushed away thoughts he found counterproductive.

He would begin his search for Vladmin in Trydon. His brother wanted to be found; the appearance of the creature made that clear. But for what purpose? What plan had Vladmin devised for his brother?

It didn't matter. Garrius would find Vladmin, and then find a way to defeat him—kill him if that's what it took. He'd always found a way before.

His mind drifted back to thoughts of Milos. The young man's power was frightening. A small part of Garrius wished that he had died on the muddy ground in front of the Old Witch's home, unable to use his magic to protect himself. But now Milos had had a glimpse of his own power; his magic had saved his life.

Garrius had left him in the care of Elder Sakrov, in the Dinuvian monastery north of Quisin. Garrius hoped that when Milos regained his consciousness and his strength, he would forget about having any more adventures and return to his kingdom and marry his princess and never think about magic again. But he couldn't believe that it would be so.

Atop his horse, Garrius Arilius rode to the village of his birth.

Part Two
Defeat

VLADMIN was nine years old the first time he snuck into Thersa's room and hid under her bed. He watched her undress, shedding layers of clothing like the fall of autumn leaves.

She caught him one day a few weeks later. He had made a sound.

"Don't scream!" he said quickly. "Please don't scream!"

"Vladmin?" She pulled a towel around her body as he crawled out from underneath the bed. "Vladmin, how could you?"

He stared at his toes and didn't say anything.

"Should I tell your father?"

"No!" Vladmin said. Then, softer: "Please, no."

She didn't tell his father; she told his brother instead.

"You did a bad thing," Garrius said. "You must have respect for other people's privacy."

"I know," Vladmin said. "It won't happen again, I promise."

When Thersa caught him the second time, Vladmin thought he was in for another of his brother's lectures. But Garrius didn't say very much this time. He just asked Vladmin to give him his word that it would never happen again, which Vladmin did. "I'm sorry, Garrius," he added. "I really am." He really was. He made a promise to himself to stay away from Thersa's room.

By the time he was thirteen, though, Vladmin had surpassed even his own teachers in the use of magic. He could not only make himself invisible, he could walk through walls. *I can visit Thersa now*, he thought. For four years, he hadn't entertained the slightest notion of going back; but now it was all he could think about.

Invisible, Vladmin snuck into her room and hid under the bed.

When Thersa finally arrived, she wasn't alone. A man was with her, and they spoke between kissing and throwing off each other's clothes.

"The wine," the man said, breathing hard. "The wine—will it be ready this week?"

"Ye—es. Tomorrow night. At the usual place."

"Tomorrow night," he repeated, his words punctuated by loud, wet kisses. "At the usual place."

"Make sure," Thersa began, then paused to moan. "Make sure. Make sure you have all the money this time. All the money, or you get none of the wine."

Still invisible, Vladmin snuck out from underneath the bed and left the room, walking through the door. It was now his turn to tattle to Garrius.

"I'll speak with her," Garrius said.

"Speak with her? Put your sword through her!"

"That's not how we deal with problems, Vladmin. I'll speak with her."

"But she's cheating our father! She's stealing from the king!"

"I'll take care of it."

Although Garrius was only fifteen, only two years older, he treated Vladmin like a child.

The next day, Thersa's room was bare, and Thersa herself was gone. Their father would never have known the real reason she had left, except that Vladmin told him.

"Arrest her," the king told the captain of the High Guard. "Then have her executed." When the captain left, his father turned to Vladmin. "I'm glad you came to me with this."

Later that day, Vladmin said to his brother, "You're not the favorite son anymore."

Garrius was exercising outside, doing push-ups on top of one of the castle walls.

"Fine by me," he said distractedly.

"You're lying. You don't have any aptitude for magic. I do. And since he found out, father has given me more attention than he ever gave you. It makes you mad."

"It makes me mad when you use your powers to spy on people, Vladmin. As for father's attention, I'm happy to let you have it."

"Thersa's dead."

Garrius finally stopped moving, his extended arms holding him up, and turned to look at his brother. "What?"

"Or she will be. Father has ordered her execution."

"No."

Vladmin nodded.

Without another word, Garrius leapt off the wall and burst through the doorway leading to the stairwell.

Vladmin took a deep breath and sank through the floor. He was waiting for Garrius in the Throne Room.

"You must call off the execution," Garrius said.

"Careful, son." Staring down from his throne, the king looked like a talking statue of a terrible, scowling giant. "Never presume to tell me what I must do."

"*Please* call off the execution. I beg of you."

"It is too late." Garrius's eyes grew wide. "I have already spoken."

Garrius stood unmoving before the throne for a long moment, hardly blinking.

Perhaps he dreams of defying our father, Vladmin thought; *perhaps he dreams of becoming king himself.*

But the moment passed, and Garrius turned and left without a word.

The king motioned for Vladmin to come closer. "Your powers have improved greatly. You can pass through material objects now."

"Yes." Vladmin knew what his father was thinking: even the best of the king's magicians couldn't walk through walls.

His father put his hand on Vladmin's shoulder. "This room is protected by powerful magic."

"I didn't know that."

The king nodded. "You broke through the protective barrier. Without even noticing."

Vladmin saw in his father's eyes something that he'd never seen there before.

My powers have grown indeed, he thought; *grown so much that my own father fears me.* Vladmin cherished the thought.

Soon there weren't many left, on the castle grounds or in the neighboring villages, who didn't fear Vladmin. His father's country was his playground, and his father's people his playthings. When he was fourteen,

Vladmin turned himself into a monster, eight feet tall, with one giant eye and four arms and teeth like jagged rocks. He stomped through a village near the castle, screaming "Argh!" and "Ugh!" at the terrified villagers. It was hilarious. But Garrius didn't think so.

"This has to stop."

Vladmin was in his room, healing a minor wound an over-zealous villager with a bow and arrow and good aim had put in his chest. (That villager woke the next day to discover he'd lost his sight.)

"Does it?" Vladmin said. "Father wants me to develop my powers."

"You can develop your powers without terrorizing people."

"But where's the fun in that?" Vladmin said, but Garrius didn't find that funny either.

They had been close, once. So close that some people joked that Vladmin was like a puppy, leashed to Garrius. *What happened?* But he knew: *Priscilla happened.* And it was his fault that Garrius and Priscilla ever met.

One day a few months earlier, Vladmin had flown through a nearby village in the shape of a small bird, looking for women he wanted to see naked. He found one. She was in the yard behind her home, hanging clothes on a length of rope stretched between two trees. She was young, perhaps only a year or two older than him. And she was beautiful.

He returned that night, but she was already in bed. He returned the next night, at an earlier time, and watched her take a bath. It was worth the wait. She was so beautiful that Vladmin couldn't stop watching her, even though staying invisible for so long was draining.

His tiredness, he would decide later, was why she'd gotten the better of him. When she stepped out of the bath and seemed to be reaching for the towel, he didn't think anything of it. But then, with amazing speed, she had crossed the distance between them, pushed him to the ground, and held a knife against his face.

Startled, he lost his concentration and turned visible.

Her knife dropped to his throat before recognition set in. When it did, her eyes grew wide and she said, "Prince Vladmin?"

Instead of answering, Vladmin took a deep breath and sank through the floor. Her father—a large, muscled man—was bounding up the stairs, looking so purposeful that it was obvious he'd heard something. Vladmin was glad he'd turned invisible again.

More nervous and afraid than a prince should ever be, he ran out of the house and returned to the castle.

Garrius is going to kill me. But he hoped that the young woman and her father knew their place enough that they wouldn't come to the castle to complain. *Why didn't I stop her tongue?* He'd been startled, that's why; he'd just wanted to get out of there.

The very next day, Vladmin walked out of a conference with his father to find the young woman among those waiting in the entrance hall for an audience with the king. Vladmin had one of the guards remove her from the line and throw her out of the castle.

"Don't come back," he told her. "My mercy has its limits."

In the yard just inside the gates, Garrius was training some of the king's soldiers. Vladmin usually loved to watch Garrius fight with a sword; he was so good that five or six of them would attack him, and before any of the soldiers could blink twice, they'd all been disarmed and laid flat on their backs. But on that particular day, Vladmin cursed his brother's presence.

The girl struggled against the guard dragging her towards the gates, and the commotion attracted Garrius's attention. Vladmin flashed a reassuring smile Garrius's way, then quietly instructed the guard to get the girl off castle grounds and make sure she never returned.

They hadn't taken three steps before Garrius stopped them.

"What's your name?" With a wave of his hand, Garrius dismissed the guard.

"Priscilla." She looked straight into his eyes, as if speaking to an equal.

"What have you done?"

Feeling helpless, Vladmin watched and waited.

"What have I done? I've done nothing! I've come for an apology, and I won't leave until I've had it!"

"An apology for what?"

"I caught your brother in my room. He was watching me bathe."

"Oh," Garrius said. Then, still staring at the commoner, he said, "Vladmin, come here."

When Vladmin walked over, Garrius finally turned to look at him. "Is this true?"

Vladmin nodded, unable to stop his face from flushing.

"Apologize."

"I'm sorry," Vladmin said, too embarrassed to look at the girl. "I'm sorry."

"It won't happen again," Garrius said, cold eyes still fixed on Vladmin. "Will it?"

"No. I'm sorry."

Garrius offered to escort Priscilla back to the village; she accepted. Vladmin considered accompanying them on their walk (in disguise, of course), or at least spying on their conversation from a distance. But he'd apologized to Priscilla. He couldn't apologize one moment and do something wicked the next, could he?

Things only got worse in the following months. After that day, Garrius and Priscilla became almost inseparable. Already Garrius and Vladmin had spent the last few years drifting apart, but with Priscilla occupying most of Garrius's time, Vladmin felt like he'd completely lost his brother—to a commoner. It became so bad that Vladmin only saw his brother when Garrius was in the mood for lecturing.

Hardly more than a year later, Garrius left, turning his back on his family and on his brother. It was Priscilla's fault, Vladmin knew; Priscilla who had never liked him and had never respected him.

Before they'd left, Vladmin had forbidden Priscilla from marrying his brother. But she didn't care; in addition to not liking or respecting him, Priscilla was foolish enough to not fear him either. Perhaps she wasn't in awe of his powers because her first experience of his magic had her seeing past his invisibility somehow. Or perhaps she felt that her hero-husband Garrius could protect her from anything. Either way, she was a fool. *I will kill you, Priscilla.*

But, over time, his anger abated. There were more interesting things to think about than Garrius and his commoner wife. *Forget about them,* he finally told himself. *Garrius doesn't want you in his life, and you don't want him in yours.*

It didn't work out that way.

M Y brother is coming for me," Vladmin said, many years later. "He is coming for me, and he intends to end my life."

"Prince Garrius is coming here?" Nanthos didn't make the slightest attempt to mask the terror in his eyes and in his voice.

Vladmin couldn't help but wonder at that. Because he knew he had Vladmin's protection, Nanthos had never shown any signs of fear before. But even he trembled at the thought of Garrius Arilius. Mighty Garrius Arilius, who defeated small armies in the morning and freed villages from evil tyrants in the afternoon. Mighty Garrius Arilius, who faced spells and swords, curses and claws, magicians and monsters, and always came out the victor.

"We knew this would happen," Nanthos said, getting up from the table and pacing. "We've gone too far. His ears could stay deaf to the people's cries for only so long."

"Quiet, fool. Have I ever failed to protect you before?"

"You've never had to protect me from your brother," Nanthos said. "We must tell the king."

"My father is ill."

Nanthos gave him a look as if to say, *You're the one who made him ill; make him better.*

"My father is ill," Vladmin repeated.

"Garrius has never lost a battle. Nothing has ever stopped him, not even the greatest magicians."

"Careful, Nanthos. I am not your local village wizard. I have more power in one fingernail than all of those fools combined."

"Garrius is protected by a greater power. There is no magic in the world that can stop him."

Nanthos had sunk back into his chair at the table, his face buried in his hands. He didn't see the look of disgust Vladmin shot at him.

"Do not buy the lies the rabble tells itself, Nanthos. Garrius is a man. If we cut his flesh, he will bleed. If we pierce his heart, he will die."

"The rabble may know more than you give them credit for," Nanthos said, raising his head to look at Vladmin. "How else do you explain your brother's success?"

"Attitudes like yours go a long way, I should think. Garrius has usually won the fight before he's removed his coat. But not with me."

"You're going to fight him?"

"I love my brother. I would have let him live in peace, him and that dog-wife of his. I didn't ask for this fight. Garrius comes to me." He kept staring at his friend. *Soon you will fear me as you fear him, Nanthos. This world will fear Vladmin all the more, when Vladmin destroys Mighty Garrius Arilius.*

A chill swept through him. He closed his eyes, then opened them again almost immediately.

"Garrius is at the gates."

IT'S been too long, brother." Vladmin's words didn't sound as cold or aggressive as he'd intended. Although he'd used his powers to watch Garrius many times through the years, seeing him now with his own eyes was different.

Atop his horse, Garrius looked stately, a golden statue carved by a master sculptor. His eyes were as sharp as ever, and they surveyed Vladmin calmly. Garrius had known much fear in his life, but always at second remove and never in his own breast.

"Not long enough, for what I have to do," Garrius said. For a moment his gaze broke from Vladmin's and he looked past him at their old home. Vladmin could almost hear his thoughts: *the castle is much changed from what I last remember. Much changed, and not for the better.* Garrius probably thought the same of his brother.

"Although I am surprised to see you," Garrius said. "Most tyrants hide behind their walls and their soldiers for as long as possible."

"Then perhaps you are mistaken about me. Perhaps I am not a tyrant."

"Perhaps." Garrius alighted from his horse and took a step towards Vladmin. "But in that case, there is another in this world who has assumed your powers and is causing great harm in your name. This man isn't content to slay his enemies, but their innocent children too."

Vladmin took a step back before he could stop himself. *He's just a man. Pierce him and he'll bleed.*

"Innocent children grow into guilty kings," Vladmin said.

"Yes," Garrius said, his gaze sweeping over his brother from top to bottom. "I know. But your tyranny ends today."

"Careful, brother. Arrogance alone will not win you a fight, and is more likely to cause the opposite result. But tell me something: who are you to right wrongs with wrongs? Who are you to ride throughout the world and attack others for attacking others? Where are the scales with which you weigh your actions against theirs, to ensure always that your wrongs are lighter than the ones of those whose lives you've taken?"

"No scales but my conscience and my prayers. Before a battle, I ask Thephis for one thing only: if I am right, let me be victorious; if I am wrong, forgive me and let me die with honor. When was the last time you prayed, Vladmin?"

"Prayed, brother? To whom shall I pray? I am more powerful than any god I can imagine."

"Before the sun sets, I will show you that you are not so powerful as you suppose."

"So no mercy from Garrius the Mighty? Or is it Garrius the Mercenary? There are hefty rewards for my head, I know. Are you here on your own, or is your sword hired by someone too cowardly to face me?"

"On my own," Garrius said. "As for mercy, I am always amazed that those who have never shown it to anyone else instantly invoke it for themselves."

"I invoke nothing!"

Garrius paused before answering. Was there doubt in his eyes? Now that the time had come, did he wonder if he could kill his own brother?

"I have waited my whole life for you to stop using your powers to hurt others, Vladmin. But every year news of your evil acts reaches my ears. Every year your abuses have grown, in number and extreme. Your evils feed on themselves. The more there are, the larger their appetite."

All these years and still with the lectures. "There is more blood on your hands than on mine," Vladmin said. "But what of that? My own brother has come for my life. Tyrant or not, Garrius, I would never turn on my own flesh and blood."

Before he spoke the last word, Garrius's eyes narrowed and an accusing, humorless smile played on his lips.

"Our father is ill of natural causes," Vladmin said, anger swelling up inside of him.

"For all your sins, you never were much of a liar."

With a loud yell, Vladmin pushed his hands together and out, sending a debilitating wave of pain towards his brother. But Garrius was no longer there, and the wave hit his horse instead. The animal fell to the ground, in so much agony that it couldn't utter the barest whisper of a scream. Its eyes bulged bigger and bigger until its entire muscled body gave one last spasm and then lay still.

Vladmin fell as Garrius collided into him.

"You killed her!" Garrius said, towering over Vladmin. His brother's voice was full of so much anguish that if Vladmin weren't afraid of him before, he was terrified now. "It will be the last life you take!"

Despite having the wind knocked out of him, Vladmin managed to concentrate long enough to turn himself into a small snake as green as the grass that surrounded them. He slithered behind Garrius and rose from the ground, transforming back into himself. As Garrius turned around, Vladmin bound his brother with thick rope that flowed from the outstretched fingers of his raised hands and wrapped itself around Garrius in tightening circles down his body.

"Did you really think you could kill me?" Vladmin walked up to the bound Garrius and pushed him to the ground. "Your horse, you yourself . . . and then, can you guess who next?" Garrius's eyes flared in anger.

Vladmin leaned over to whisper in his ear. "That's right. I would have left her alone. But you came after me. First I kill you, then—"

Vladmin found himself with a mouthful of grass. Too quickly for Vladmin to stop him, Garrius had twisted and flung his lower body and kicked Vladmin over.

The ropes had dissolved as soon as Vladmin lost his concentration. Garrius was free, free enough to pull out his sword and press its cold steel against the back of Vladmin's neck.

I'm dead, he thought.

But he wasn't. Garrius had hesitated, was hesitating still. Mighty Garrius Arilius, merciful after all. *It will be the death of you.* Vladmin sent another wave of pain straight up.

Garrius stumbled backward, fell. He lay on the ground, curled up and clutching his sides, as if by applying pressure he could stop the pain. *You'll squeeze out your life before you squeeze out the pain, brother.*

Vladmin looked up and saw his people—guards and soldiers and servants—watching from the top of the the castle walls, in defiance of his orders to stay hidden.

"Behold," Vladmin said, amplifying his voice so that it boomed. "Behold Garrius the Mighty, squirming at my feet like a dying worm. My brother came for my life and found his own death instead. So it is with anyone who dares cross me!"

But Garrius wasn't dying. Vladmin turned to look at him—his strength was hard to believe. No one before had ever survived this long against the agonizing pain tearing through their body, biting at their flesh like a ravenous animal.

Vladmin held up his hand and Garrius stopped

squirming. He lay spread out on the grass, sweat on his face and blood dripping from his ears and nostrils.

"My brother will not die today," he said. "A quick death is too kind for those who oppose me."

A change in the faces of some in the crowd made Vladmin turn around. Garrius had gotten to his feet, his sword in his hand. He was hunched over and his steps were slow and deliberate, but he was on his feet.

Vladmin sent another wave of pain. Garrius fell to the ground as if hit by a stampeding horse, but in the next instant he was on his feet again. It shouldn't have been possible. Vladmin sent another wave, and then another. They slowed Garrius down, but neither was capable of stopping him or sending him back to the ground. Vladmin could feel Garrius's mind resisting the magic.

My power is leaving me; I'm panicking. I must stay focused.

Garrius was in front of him. With his left hand he grabbed Vladmin's tunic, and with his right he pressed his sword's tip against Vladmin's chest, above his heart. Frozen by fear, Vladmin stared into his brother's eyes.

In one motion, Garrius pulled with his left arm and pushed with his right. Vladmin screamed as the steel pierced his flesh; the sound filled the air and must have been heard up to the far end of the castle. His cry of pain was met by cheering and applause from the castle, as the traitorous rabble felt safe enough to proclaim in public what they had feared, mere hours before, to so much as whisper in private.

Garrius staggered back a few steps, then fell to the ground, unconscious.

Breathing with effort, Vladmin dulled the pain, starting at either end of the wound and moving deeper into his body. With both hands, he grabbed the hilt of the sword. He pulled—once, then paused to rest; twice, and the sword was out. He turned around. From the castle, startled eyes met his gaze. Without a word, Vladmin threw his brother's sword towards the castle, then made the blade burst into dozens of sharp pieces. Flying through the air and through walls, the small steel daggers pierced the throats that moments ago had yelled their pleasure at Vladmin's supposed demise.

The spell proved too much for him; Vladmin dropped to his knees. He was losing a lot of blood, and the pain was held at bay only by great effort. He fell flat on the ground, his breathing slow and raspy. His head was swimming; he felt himself sinking into unconsciousness and back out again, like a drowning animal tossed by waves above and below the water's surface.

He felt hands on him, turning him over. His vision was blurred. Who was it? Garrius, come to finish what he'd started?

"It'll be all right," he heard a voice tell him. Nanthos! *Good, faithful Nanthos!*

"Help me," Vladmin said. "Help me, or I will die."

"Tell me what to do."

"There are salt crystals in my room—in the chest at the foot of my bed—in a small blue pouch. Bring them here. Rub them into my wound."

"I can't leave you. It isn't safe."

"Garrius?"

"Garrius is gone. They carried him into the castle. But they'll return. For you."

"My own people?"

"You killed their loved ones; their corpses fill the castle. My sword—and fear that you aren't as helpless as you look—have kept them away for now."

"You must carry me, then." Vladmin felt arms going underneath him, struggling to pull him up. "I'm sorry, my friend. I don't have the strength to make your burden light."

"I will manage."

More than once, Vladmin blacked out, losing the fight to remain conscious only to be jostled back as Nanthos's rough handling turned rougher. Nanthos made slow progress, half-carrying and half-dragging his charge. Later, he pushed Vladmin off of him; Vladmin fell, but landed on something soft. It was only then that he realized they'd reached his room, and that he lay on his own bed.

"Quickly, my friend," Vladmin said.

He heard the chest open, heard Nanthos rummaging around, looking for the small pouch. Soon it wouldn't matter. . . Vladmin would be dead and no amount of salt crystals or any other magic could bring him back.

He woke at the slight discomfort he experienced when Nanthos placed the crystals on his wound.

"You must push them in, as far as—"

Vladmin screamed as Nanthos did so and the pain, like hottest fire, burned through his body. But after a few moments, the scorching pain cooled and he started to feel better. His breathing became easier and—he felt around with his fingers—the wound in his chest had started to heal over.

"What do we do now?"

Vladmin pushed himself off the bed, but collapsed to the floor. "I need time to rest."

Nanthos helped him up. Vladmin closed his eyes and searched for Garrius, his brow furrowing with concentration. "Garrius is well," he said, hardly able to believe it himself. "He is evacuating the castle."

"Your father?"

"My brother is leaving no one behind."

"Garrius leaves with them?"

"Don't sound so hopeful, fool."

"We must escape," Nanthos said, grabbing Vladmin and almost tipping him over. "Before it's too late, we must escape." Vladmin tried to break the grip, but Nanthos wouldn't let him go. "We all saw it. Garrius resisted your power. He ran his sword through you, and you were helpless to stop him."

"Coward," Vladmin said, finally breaking the other's hold. He stood straighter. "Garrius is only a man."

"So are you."

"I will kill Garrius," Vladmin said, his eyes wide open now and unblinking. He took a deep breath, as if drawing in power along with air. "And then I will chase down the traitorous scum who've abandoned me and, one by one, I will kill them too."

IN the courtyard where they used to play together, Garrius waited for Vladmin. He sat on the ground on crossed legs, his eyes closed.

"Vladmin," Garrius said.

"Perhaps my magic-hating brother has powers of his own."

"Learning to listen is not magic." Garrius opened his eyes and rose to his feet.

"It wasn't enough to abandon me yourself?" Vladmin said. "It wasn't enough to turn your back on your own family for a commoner? You had to chase away my own people?"

"Earlier today I helped carry the bodies of dozens of your own people."

"Traitors, all! Why did they cheer when they thought me dead?"

"It was the end of your tyranny they cheered, Vladmin. But not all were traitors, I see."

Vladmin turned; Nanthos was hiding (poorly) behind one of the marble columns in the courtyard. Seeing that he was discovered, he stepped out from behind the column and said, "King Vladmin is my friend, Prince Garrius. And one day he will rule the world."

"And what about you?" Garrius said.

"Nanthos is my most trusted advisor," Vladmin said. "And my closest friend. Today he even saved my life. The rewards he's received from my hand will be as nothing compared to the ones he will receive."

At these words, Nanthos beamed.

"And if Vladmin should fall today?" Garrius said, still addressing Nanthos. "Will you also share in his fate?"

Before the coward could betray himself, Vladmin said, "Do not let this morning's battle amplify your arrogance, brother. I was unprepared for your attack—"

"You attacked me," Garrius said, quietly.

"—and unwilling to unleash my full power on you. But now? You should have escaped with your treacherous mob." Before Garrius could respond, Vladmin continued, "But that you should know—even with your dying breath—the extent of my power, I fight you now on your own terms, with your own chosen weapon, in this courtyard where you once trained." With that, he extended his right arm, except it was no longer his arm but a sword the width and length of his own body and yet weighing almost nothing. Garrius's sword, borrowed from one of the runaway soldiers or stolen from a corpse, was short and thin and pathetic in comparison.

With what he hoped was a sudden leap forward, Vladmin swung. Garrius pulled his disappearing trick again, though, and wasn't where he'd been: he'd rolled forward, past Vladmin, and come up behind him. Vladmin brought his sword up just in time to block Garrius's attack.

Without wasting a moment, Garrius charged forward, striking with his free hand, sending Vladmin reeling to the ground. As Vladmin fell, he lost his concentration and the sword disappeared.

Garrius was upon him once again. The tip of his sword pressed on the base of Vladmin's throat—Vladmin took a quick breath and disappeared, not willing to find out if his brother would hesitate again.

"By my terms, opponents don't vanish when they're losing," Garrius said, looking around.

Vladmin struck him from behind; Garrius stumbled a few steps, but kept to his feet. Gathering his power to give himself amplified speed and strength, Vladmin swallowed up the distance between them, picked up Garrius, and threw him against one of the marble columns. Garrius collapsed to the ground, looking like a discarded rag doll.

Nanthos was gone. Perhaps sensing the battle was lost, Vladmin thought, the coward had escaped. Vladmin closed his eyes, unable to resist the temptation of his curiosity. Nanthos was climbing stairs towards the balcony above the entrance to the courtyard, presumably so he could watch the battle from a safer distance.

Vladmin's eyes flew open as a strong grip tightened around his throat. Garrius held Vladmin with his right hand; with his left, he pushed his thumb against the side of Vladmin's neck, at the base. The effect was excruciating, blinding, incapacitating pain.

Vladmin fought past it. He raised his skin's temperature, higher and higher, until touching him shouldn't have been possible. But Garrius ignored it, as if his own skin weren't being burned, and kept squeezing with one hand and applying pressure with the other.

"You're dead unless I let you go," Garrius said, whispering into Vladmin's ear. "Swear to Thephis that you'll never use magic again; do that and I'll let you live."

"Ye—es." He nodded as much as Garrius's grip would allow. "Ple—ease. I swear, Garrius."

His brother let him go. His hands were pink, raw from having the skin burned off, but he managed to look relieved.

"I can heal that for you," Vladmin said with a laugh, allowing his temperature to drop and rubbing his throat.

Garrius smiled despite the pain. "Very funny."

"How sad." Vladmin raised his hand.

Garrius started coughing. His left hand reached up to his throat, as if to break Vladmin's hold.

Stepping away from him, Vladmin said, "How sad that my own brother knows me not at all. You have no idea how disappointing that is."

Garrius stumbled back, but—too late!—Vladmin noticed how he'd moved in a deliberate and unnatural way. Garrius fell to the ground, grabbed the sword he'd dropped when Vladmin had flung him against the column, and sent it spinning end-over-end, directly at Vladmin, right into the wound that was still healing. It all happened as if in one motion. Vladmin was amazed: Garrius had always been fast, but how could he—unable to breathe, choking to death, blinded by tears—move so quickly or aim so truly? Despite all of Vladmin's powers, Garrius had bested him; not once, but at least twice now.

Vladmin didn't try to pull out the sword that had run through him, and might have kept going right out the other side if not for the hilt. The pain was horrible, even worse than the first time, but he couldn't summon the energy to numb it. *Bested by Garrius*, he couldn't help but think, *despite all of my powers*. Garrius the Mighty indeed, who could name Vladmin as yet another vanquished foe, and perhaps not the greatest of those either.

Garrius's scream recalled his attention—Garrius was hurt! But how? By whom?

Nanthos! From the balcony, Nanthos had thrown his own sword; although neither his aim nor his strength were equal to Garrius's, his weapon had struck Garrius's upper thigh. It stuck out like a flag planted in conquered soil.

The sight infused Vladmin with new energy. He numbed the pain, pulled out the sword, then floated to the balcony to stand beside Nanthos.

Garrius easily rolled away from the first collapsing column Vladmin sent his way; the second missed him by only a hair, but still it missed him. Vladmin didn't have a third chance: Garrius rolled into the entrance, armed with the sword he'd pulled from his own leg.

Vladmin closed his eyes, collapsed the stairs in front of Garrius, but saw him leap the rest of the way.

"He's coming for us."

"Stop him!" Nanthos's voice was hysterical.

"I can't," Vladmin said, his eyes still closed. The spells had taken a lot out of him, and in his weakened state he didn't feel he had anything left to give. "I'm so tired."

"Not too tired to save your life, I hope!" Nanthos tackled Vladmin and together they tumbled over the railing.

When Garrius burst onto the balcony, Vladmin and Nanthos were on the courtyard ground, unharmed by the fall. Garrius wasn't so lucky; no sooner had he stepped onto the platform but Vladmin made it collapse. Garrius jumped from the falling stones in mid-air, aiming for a patch of soft grass. He landed well and wouldn't have suffered from the fall, except that Vladmin helped a stray piece hit its mark. Garrius was struck from behind just below the neck and knocked onto the ground. Although Vladmin had been aiming higher, weak as he was, he was pleased to have hit Garrius at all.

"Quickly now," Vladmin said. "Garrius stirs even as we stand watching."

The pair stumbled into the entrance to the castle, Vladmin relying almost entirely on Nanthos to keep him upright and moving. The thought gripped him that at any moment Nanthos might decide to abandon Vladmin to save his own life. He'd been abandoned by everyone else, why not Nanthos? When Nanthos leaned him against a wall, Vladmin was convinced he was being sacrificed, a gift to appease the great god Garrius.

There is energy in me to kill you yet, false friend. He gathered his powers. But Nanthos had run up to a decorative hanging, a golden shield against which two ceremonial swords were strapped. He released one of the swords, then sheathed it.

Vladmin relaxed, and almost immediately felt a stabbing pain in his chest. It was but a shadow of the full pain, held back by the faltering guard of his dwindling power, ready to rush in and overwhelm him as soon as his concentration waned.

Nanthos returned and slipped an arm underneath

Vladmin's, transferring the burden from the wall to himself.

"Stay," Vladmin said. He fixed his gaze on the piece of ceiling above the entrance. At length it began to tremble, then to shake, then to crumble. Stones fell into a heap that sealed the entrance. Vladmin almost collapsed himself, but Nanthos held him up.

They went from room to room, stopping long enough to seal the doorway behind them. But where would it end? Garrius would eventually break through the seals, or find another way to reach them. Garrius would pursue Vladmin until his brother was dead; the great hunter wouldn't stop until he'd chased down his prey and killed it.

If only he could escape from Garrius's pursuit, he thought, to hide and recover his powers. If only he could win a reprieve, postpone their battle for a later date.

"Garrius!" Nanthos's voice was loud, and full of fear and surprise.

Vladmin looked up; sure enough, his brother stood before them, having taken a shortcut Vladmin thought only he knew existed, having bypassed the obstacles Vladmin had put in his path at no little cost.

Infuriated, Vladmin reached across to Nanthos's scabbard. In one motion, he pulled out and threw the sword, then helped direct it towards Garrius's heart. But his brother easily deflected the attack with his own sword. What's more, he spun it with the deflection and grabbed its hilt with his free hand. Now he had two swords. Vladmin tried to wrestle it free with his powers, but to no avail. Garrius's grip—both that of his hand and that of his mind—proved too strong.

You will not rest until one of us is dead, Vladmin

thought, *but must it be me?*

Another thought occurred to him then, and he suddenly looked over at the fear-stricken Nanthos.

Above them, the ceiling trembled and shook and crumbled. Garrius dove out of the way, but not so Nanthos. Directed by Vladmin's power, a piece of the ceiling fell on him, knocking Nanthos to the ground; another piece fell and crushed his lower body. He lay dying. Out of friendship, Vladmin kneeled beside him and sealed his mouth and nose. Soon Nanthos was dead.

When the ceiling had stopped crumbling and the dust had settled, Garrius stood before him.

"Vladmin is dead," Vladmin said, standing up. At his feet lay Nanthos's half-crushed body, which looked in every way like Vladmin's half-crushed body.

Garrius stared at the dead man. For a moment, Vladmin feared he might see through the deception. But Garrius eventually broke his gaze and fixed it on Vladmin again. "You were his friend?"

"Perhaps his only friend," Vladmin said, speaking slowly. The pain at his chest, the trouble of keeping his voice sounding like Nanthos's, the cost of keeping up the illusion on both bodies—it all wore on him. He didn't know how long he could last. "Will you kill me now too?"

"You're hurt."

"I will live, if you do not kill me."

"If you promise to do no evil, from this day until you die, I will not kill you."

"I promise."

"If events should prove otherwise—"

"I have given my word," Vladmin said. He felt himself about to faint.

Garrius started pushing the stone off of Nanthos's body, but Vladmin stopped him.

"We must bury him," Garrius said.

Vladmin shook his head. "Allow me the honor. Allow me this last task of a dutiful friend."

Garrius hesitated. "This is what I came to do. But I have no pleasure in it. My brother is dead, my father's castle is in ruins, my father himself so near death when I last saw him that he may have perished along the road."

"Go to him," Vladmin said, anxious for Garrius to leave, terrified that he'd lose his hold on the various spells before then.

Garrius kneeled beside Nanthos's body. Vladmin forced himself to remain calm.

"Goodbye, brother." Garrius bent over and kissed Nanthos on the forehead. "I truly wish it had ended otherwise between us. May Thephis have mercy on your soul."

He stood and, with a parting nod to Vladmin, he limped out of the room.

V LADMIN had won, Garrius had lost. *Mighty Garrius failed to kill me.* Vladmin had gained the reprieve he'd wanted; he'd gained the time to rest and recover—as much time as he needed, safe from Garrius until he chose to reveal himself.

Because Vladmin had never encountered a mind as strong as his brother's. Garrius was too confident, too focused, his conscience far too clear.

I will feed you meal after meal of defeat and doubt, Vladmin thought. *I will strip away your commoner wife, your overpowering confidence in yourself, your mighty strength, and finally—but not until you've suf-fered sufficiently first—I will take that which you came to take from me: your very life.*

These thoughts, and more like them, were Vlad-min's only company as he healed from the many wounds he'd suffered at Garrius's hands. When he was fit for travel, he went to a distant land in the far north, where he could use and grow his powers without fear that news of his actions would reach Garrius's ears.

In that distant land, in a small hill castle he took for his own, Vladmin spent many days upon his captured throne, thoughts of revenge heavy on his mind.

Part Three
Victory

THE village of his youth was dead, as dead as he'd left it. Deader even, although ironically the lack of inhabitants which made Garrius think Trydon so desolate had allowed for an explosion of vegetative life as weeds erupted through the cracks in the cobblestone streets and around the run-down houses.

What had he expected? The last few inhabitants who refused to leave their homes even if it meant enduring his brother's tyranny had likely died off by now—or, if he wanted to think more optimistically, had finally consented to leave once Garrius was supposed to have killed Vladmin and his brother's kingdom collapsed.

Garrius tried to push away the feelings of guilt and, as he entered the forest at the edge of the village along the wide and well-worn path that was also showing signs of being reclaimed by nature, he readied himself for the sight of the ruins of his old home. Garrius had left quickly after his brother's death, only to find that the hurried journey away from the castle had claimed their father's life. He'd tried in every way to distance himself from the memories of that day. Perhaps for that reason, he hadn't thought very much until now about the reports of intrepid kings and merchants who had raided what was left of their castle to steal away what they could, including the very stones from its walls.

He'd left Asher in a stable in the farm house of friends who lived in the countryside not far from the village, with instructions and money to care for his horse if he didn't return. He'd patted Asher's face and told him it was safer for him to stay there, but now he almost wished he had company as he returned to face Vladmin, as selfish as he knew that was.

Lost in his thoughts, he came to the edge of the forest and began to climb towards the towering castle almost unconsciously, not realizing until he was at the gates that this wasn't how things should be. Eyes wide, he stepped into the courtyard; the path was lined with rows of well-trimmed trees leading to the wooden doors as large as three men one atop the other, both of which stood as open as the gates. Far from being in ruins, the castle gleamed in the noon sun's light. Baskets of red and orange and white flowers hung from the balconies (Vladmin's mother had been an avid gardener).

Two guards in full uniform stood on either side of the entrance. They ignored Garrius. He walked up the stone steps in disbelief and into the marble hallway. A sudden headache made him wince; he paused, and the sharp pain passed, but left behind it a feeling of nausea he wasn't accustomed to.

After a moment, he forced himself to keep walking. Even the shock of seeing the castle exactly as it had been, though, couldn't have prepared him for the sight of his brother, who stood at the other end of the hall wearing their father's crown and a fur-lined purple robe. Uniformed soldiers surrounded him on both sides and Garrius saw several more behind him.

"Welcome home, Garrius," Vladmin said. Then he

laughed heartily and said, "Turn and look at your expression in that mirror!"

Although his brother's voice was full of derision, Garrius still felt himself strangely moved. He'd thought Vladmin dead—by Garrius's own hands, no less—and yet there he stood, alive, resplendent in his regal attire and bejeweled crown, looking as healthy and strong as Garrius had ever seen him. The thin features of his face were still pulled tight though, as if in constant tension or anger. His dark eyes were narrowed in concentration, perhaps waiting to see if Garrius would try to attack him right away.

"How did you do this?" Garrius said. "Is it real?"

Vladmin laughed again, then bowed mockingly to his brother. "You pay my powers a great compliment. This is no illusion—it is less trouble to rebuild the traditional way."

"You mean slave labor," Garrius said, a hard edge finally entering his tone.

Vladmin took a step forward, and his retinue of soldiers kept pace. "Did you return for another lecture? Or a debate on politics and economics? I thought you were here to exact vengeance for the death of your dog-wife?"

Immediately the great conflict in Garrius's mind—guilt and sadness at abandoning the castle and the villages because he had no interest in ruling himself; bewilderment at the Old Witch's revelation that his brother hadn't actually died, despite Garrius having seen Vladmin's crushed body with his own eyes; reluctance at having to engage his brother once again in battle; awe at the restored castle—all of it cleared away. Even the feeling of nausea and dizziness passed.

Garrius unsheathed his sword. "I thought I killed

you once before. I'll leave you dead and buried for good this time." Still he couldn't stop himself from adding, "If you force me to."

Again Vladmin and his entourage took a step towards Garrius. "Would you spare my life, then? After the old hag told you I was responsible for your wife's death?"

"If I thought you'd suddenly grown a conscience and would be willing to spend the rest of your life atoning for your crimes, yes. If I believed there was something in this world capable of breaking through the stone wall that imprisons your heart, yes. I've held out that hope for every tyrant I've encountered, though none were as bad as you. And yet I hold out that hope for you more than for any of the others. You're my brother, and the thought of having to fight you again is repulsive to me. But I will fight you if I have to. And I will kill you."

As he spoke, Garrius had been taking his own steps towards his brother. Now he stood within striking distance of Vladmin, which is where he liked to be when facing off against a magician. He wished his head were clearer, though; he'd never experienced anything like this, and started to wonder if it were one of Vladmin's spells, designed to make Garrius feel nauseous and unbalanced.

Vladmin closed the gap between them even further, grabbed Garrius's shoulders and leaned in to whisper in one ear: "I have a secret to share with you. It would be incautious to kill me before I've done so."

Garrius physically pushed Vladmin away from him. "I have no interest in your games," he said. "You wanted my attention, now you have it—although I dare say you'll come to regret not allowing me to think you dead and living out the rest of your miserable life making others miserable with your cruelty and greed."

"No, no," Vladmin said, "I tried that. And this is much more interesting. My one regret is that I wasn't there to see your face in person as you watched your wronged and wronging wife suffer and die. Hold it!"

Vladmin raised his hand and Garrius felt his right arm go numb as he tried to bring his sword to Vladmin's throat. One of his soldiers stepped forward and removed Garrius's weapon from his suddenly lax grip.

"I haven't shared my secret yet," Vladmin went on nonchalantly. "But first I have a question for you: was it worth it to betray and abandon your own brother for a peasant woman?"

"Don't talk about her," Garrius said, studying his brother's face for the slightest sign of waning concentration.

"But how can I not talk about her? *She's* my secret!"

Garrius waited, kept studying Vladmin's face, kept trying to move his increasingly unresponsive body.

"He's so dense," Vladmin said, turning to one of the soldiers. "He still doesn't understand." He faced his brother again. "Garrius, your peasant wife isn't dead yet. She's alive. I just told you that my one regret was not being able to see your face with my own eyes as your wife suffered and died. Don't you understand that a magician as powerful as I am does not have to live life with any regrets?"

Although he tried to tell himself to ignore Vladmin, Garrius found the temptation to believe him too strong. Could it be true? Could Priscilla still be alive?

"I saw her die," he couldn't help himself from saying.

"You saw her devoured by my pet, the great snake Orobo, who you butchered." Vladmin shrugged. "Certainly that could've meant her death, except that I protected her."

"For what purpose?"

"Dense, dense, dense. To kill her again and be able to see your face this time!"

"You're lying." Garrius's voice was faint, from the headache or the desire to not reveal how desperately he wanted Vladmin's words to be true, he wasn't sure. "You're—" The pain was too much to handle; the feeling of nausea seemed to sweep his whole body and he felt cold sweats breaking out along his skin. His vision went dark.

"Is this your doing, Vladmin?" he managed to say, before collapsing on the cold marble floor of his youth.

HE came awake in a small, dim cell of three stone walls and a fourth one of metal bars. The back wall was interrupted near the ceiling by a wide but short window. If this were anywhere in the palace, he'd never seen it before.

The pain in his head was present, but much fainter.

He sat up on the stone bed built into the side wall like a cantilever. Even when he stood and approached the metal bars, the area beyond them was shrouded in darkness. He tested their strength against his own, but they didn't budge.

"Vladmin!" he called out. "Coward!"

"Garrius?"

The voice stopped him cold.

"Garrius, is that you?"

At first, he didn't want to respond. If this were a trick of Vladmin's, he didn't want to give him the satisfaction of falling for it. But the desperation in Priscilla's voice was too hard to resist.

"Priscilla?"

"Yes!"

He swallowed hard. "I thought you dead."

"I thought myself dead."

"What happened?"

"I don't know," she said. Her voice came from a few feet to his left, but still he couldn't see anything beyond the metal bars of his own cell. "The last thing I remember is feeling myself being torn apart piece by piece. The pain was excruciating until I passed out. Then I woke up here. I have no idea how long ago that was—"

"—ten months," Garrius said.

"That long?" Priscilla's voice was quiet but full of sadness. She seemed to shake off the knowledge for the moment and continued: "I haven't seen anyone or heard a single human voice until just now, when you called out your brother's name."

"No one brings you food?"

"A loaf of bread and a cup of water appear just inside the bars of my cell every morning. I make them last through the day."

The promise to rescue her and set them both free died on Garrius's lips. He had to be sure this wasn't a trick. "Priscilla, I need to ask you something. It may sound odd, but please think about it and answer me, all right?"

"All right."

If this were an illusion, Garrius thought, it was a very good one. The inflection—suspicious, half-questioning, reluctantly agreeing—was Priscilla's to the last detail.

"There is a secret that you and I share, known to no other living creature." He expected her to try and stop him, but Priscilla was silent. "I need you to speak it out loud now. Tell me who you are."

The pain in his head had returned with the force of an explosion, but Garrius ignored it and forced himself to focus on what Priscilla would say. His wife was silent for a long time. Finally—perhaps convincing herself that Garrius wouldn't ask her to do this unless he was desperate—she said, "I am Priscilla of Avalar, first daughter of Lord Jarrius and Lady Lizome."

Although that was enough for Garrius—he closed his eyes and offered words of thanksgiving to Thephis, the pain in his head all but forgotten—his wife kept speaking: "As a young teenager, I was given to be married to a prince, the son of our king's enemy and lord of the neighboring lands. Our marriage would seal the terms of the peace treaty.

"Until I met you," she continued before he could stop her, "I thought I didn't want to marry at all. But especially not him. I once saw him kick a dog because it didn't bow the knee when he passed it on the street. I don't remember if I told you that."

"No, but similar stories." Garrius felt an energy course through him the likes of which he hadn't known since Priscilla's death—or, perhaps, not since Vladmin's supposed death. For the first time since then, he felt *himself* again; and now that he felt himself, he didn't believe that metal bars and stone walls could keep him from rescuing his wife. There was hope now, and that was all Garrius needed. "So it was marry a cruel and temperamental prince," he said, "or perpetuate a bloody war." They'd spoken of her past only once, on their wedding night.

"My father said he'd honor and defend, even to the death, whatever choice I made. I think he shuddered at my marrying the prince as much as I did. But our king had blessed the treaty. And, even if the king didn't punish my family if I refused to marry, I knew that I couldn't be responsible for more war and more deaths."

Garrius pressed his head against the bars and tried again to look out to his left, but saw nothing in the darkness. "So you married him, gave him lots of vicious little babies, and drank your weight in wine each day to forget his cruelties."

"That would've been an option, except you know I never developed the taste for wine. No. I faked my own death, the terms of the peace treaty stood, and I sailed halfway across the world. Where I was taken in by the ship's captain into his house as his own daughter and where I was found by another prince who made the first one look like—" She cut herself off, then started over, "And where, halfway across the world, I met my true husband and my true prince."

In his mind, Garrius could picture the smile on his wife's face. The sudden urge to apologize to her almost overwhelmed him. But he told himself that there would be time for all of that later—if Thephis was willing, a whole lifetime to make everything up to her, to start again and be a better husband than he'd been able to be the first time, to honor his vows the way he hadn't been able to before—but first he had to get them out of these cells and out of this prison.

"Such an interesting story," a familiar voice said from behind him. "Why did you never tell me your wife was of noble blood?"

Garrius turned around. Vladmin sat on the stone bed, the golden crown on his head and the purple robe pulled tight around his body.

"Would it have made a difference?"

"Not any material difference, no. But I feel kind of stupid now that I kept calling her a peasant. I would've thought up better insults if I'd known she was nobility."

Garrius approached carefully as his brother spoke.

"That's far enough," Vladmin said, lifting his hand lazily. Garrius found himself frozen in place again, as if his body had been turned to stone from the neck down.

Vladmin leaned back against the wall. "Tomorrow morning, at dawn, Priscilla will be executed in the square. I had initially planned to have her killed outside the gates—but she is of noble blood, after all. It should be spilled on royal ground."

"Why?" Garrius said, again trying to break free of the spell that held his body immobile, again failing to flex even a muscle below his neck. "What is this game you're playing at?"

Vladmin stood straight; he seemed almost as tall as Garrius now, though he'd always been at least a head shorter.

"You did play games with me when I was very young, Garrius—I remember. But then you stopped. And yes"—Vladmin shrugged good-naturedly—"I guess this is a game too."

"And what is the point, Vladmin?"

"To hurt you. To bring as much pain on you as any human being can bear."

"So much anger," Garrius said, with genuine sadness. "It distorts your face. Where did it all come from?"

"What?" Vladmin yelled, the wrinkles in his face growing deeper as he sneered. "The brother who tried to end my life is asking why I'm angry with him? The brother who betrayed me for a woman? Is this a joke?"

"I never wanted you dead," Garrius said. "And I never betrayed you."

Vladmin shook his head, walked towards the back of the cell. "I know you believe that. But just because you're able to lie to yourself doesn't make you any less of a liar. You know, a short while after you left with that woman, when I was growing very powerful and respected in our father's house, I asked my mother about you. I asked her why you had grown to hate me, why you had chosen to side with a peasant woman against me."

"Your mother never liked me."

Vladmin continued to stare at the cell wall. "She told me she knew how much I admired you and how much I looked up to you. But she said that you would never love me back. First, because you were jealous of me, since your own mother died while giving birth to you."

"That isn't true."

"Second," Vladmin said, finally turning around but continuing as if Garrius hadn't said anything, "because you came to disapprove of father's decision to re-marry, and to resent my mother for sitting as queen where your own mother once sat."

"That isn't true either."

"And third, because you begrudged the attention our father showered on me."

Garrius couldn't help but laugh out loud. "Father was too busy waging wars to ever give me much attention. And what little he did show me—when he thought

I'd grow up to be a great soldier in his army—I was happy to let him turn on you instead."

"When he realized I had power he could use, I know. Don't worry—I never thought my mother was right about you, not once. Do you know why?"

"No, I don't." Again Garrius tried to flex his arms and again he failed to do so despite the look of relaxation or at least non-concentration that was clear on Vladmin's face even in the dim light.

"When I was about five or six," Vladmin said, "some of father's personal Guard took you out hunting. I asked if I could come and they all said no."

"I said yes?" Garrius said, surprised.

"No, of course not. You looked me right in the eyes and promised to take me hunting for my next birthday."

Garrius nodded, although he had only a vague recollection of that conversation and of that day.

"I followed you anyway. I wanted to see you shoot a boar as I'd seen you shoot the bullseye of endless targets. I was sure you'd kill twice as many as all of the others combined."

The full recollection of that day came to Garrius. Even still, he was surprised it had made such an impression on his little brother. "You were hiding in a bush," Garrius said.

"And I shifted my weight and stirred the leaves. One of the guards turned towards me and swung back his arm. I stood, paralyzed by fear except to cry out your name. But it was too late—he'd already let the spear fly."

"It wasn't too late—I stopped it."

"If you'd hesitated for even a moment, I would've been dead with a spear through my head. But you jumped in front of me and took a spear through the stomach instead."

"I'd almost forgotten that day," Garrius said.

"I never have. Before you passed out from the pain, you craned your neck to look at me and you smiled and said, 'You're all right.' Although you had a spear sticking right out the middle of you, there was a look of pure relief and joy on your face. You see, I know my mother was wrong—you loved me then, loved me more than you loved even your own life. It was that woman that turned you against your family and against me."

"Can you set me free, please?" Garrius said. "I won't attack you."

Vladmin didn't respond, but all of a sudden Garrius had to catch himself to stop from falling forward.

"Thank you." Garrius approached his brother, but stopped short of placing his hands on him. "Vladmin, this is something you've never understood. Priscilla didn't turn me against you. Your cruelty did that. Father's cruelty did that. I couldn't abide it. It had nothing to do with Priscilla."

"I don't think that's true," Vladmin said, pushing past him. "But it doesn't matter." He stopped at the bars of the cell. "I know now she was the one who sent you to kill me—I know you never would've come after me if she hadn't insisted it was your duty to stop me, after you tried to ignore the latest coward who came to beg you to ride back to Trydon and end my so-called tyranny.

"You know it too, Garrius. You never cheated on her before, did you? You never had a hard time keeping your marriage vows, until your wife pushed you into raising a sword against your own flesh and blood, and even taking your own brother's life—or so you thought."

Garrius swallowed hard and wondered what Priscilla was making of their conversation. She was being very quiet.

Vladmin passed through the metal bars as if they or he were made of nothing but mist. His voice carried back to Garrius: "You came to kill me at her bidding; now you must both pay for your crimes against me. Tomorrow you'll watch her burn and listen to her screams. Then—oh, the things I have planned for you after that."

The voice drifted off. Garrius tested the metal bars, but they were as solid and immovable as ever. He called out to his wife, but she didn't answer.

N IGHT *of the twenty-second day.*
     Garrius didn't know why he was keeping track, except that on a deep level he felt that it was the one thing staving off a complete mental breakdown.

In the past twenty-two days, Garrius had seen his wife tied to a wooden post and burned; seen her pushed onto a guillotine and beheaded; seen her shot down by a line of bowmen. Every time, he thought she'd died. A night or two later, though, he discovered her in the cell next to his, with no recollection of anything that had happened to her. Was Vladmin bringing her back from the dead each time, as he had claimed to have brought her back once before? Was her execution an illusion? Garrius didn't know, but it was definitely his wife who kept appearing in the cell next to his each time. In fact, he was running out of tests he could put to her.

No matter how hard he tried to steel himself, though, the experience shattered him every time he had to hear his wife's screams of pain, stare into her terrified eyes, watch immobile as her body trembled and shook. In part because he knew that any time might be the last time—any time might be the true execution. He always returned to his cell desperate for that first response to his calling out of her name.

It made him laugh at himself now to think of the confidence he'd felt that first day, when he'd been blindfolded and brought out to the square in front of the castle. Perhaps believing too strongly in his own legend, Garrius was convinced that he'd find a way to rescue them both. But Vladmin held him completely immobile throughout, so that Garrius couldn't even cry out to his wife. Struggle as he might to free only his vocal chords, he wasn't able to do that the first time or any other time. He sometimes wondered if he'd grown weaker or if Vladmin had grown incredibly powerful. Either way, he was no longer a match for his younger brother, and Garrius was growing weaker by the day. Every morning, Vladmin gave him just enough food and water to keep Garrius alive, but provided a regular supply of horrors so that Garrius couldn't sleep for more than an hour or two at a time.

On that night of the twenty-second day, while he lay on his stone bed, he heard a voice calling out his name. It wasn't Vladmin's or Priscilla's, but it was familiar even though he couldn't place it immediately.

The voice came from the small window set ten feet up the wall. He stood and approached the wall.

"Who's there?" he said, looking up.

"Your friend, Milos of Stannis."

"Milos?"

"You need to come with us, immediately. Your brother's spells are powerful, even as he sleeps. I don't know how long we can hold against them—and all will be lost if he wakes."

"Then help me!" Garrius said, feeling his heart leap in his chest and a darkness like a heavy cloth lift from him. It occurred to him that this was how others might have felt when he'd rescued them after they'd given up all hope. He'd always accepted their gratitude as gracefully as he could, but he hadn't until now understood how a sense of thanksgiving seemed to burst out of oneself, like a powerful torrent breaking through a dam. "My wife is here too, Milos."

There was a long pause before Milos responded. "Your wife is dead, Garrius."

"No, that was one of Vladmin's tricks. She's alive."

"There's no time for this," he heard Milos say, and Garrius wasn't sure if he spoke to himself or to someone else. "Priscilla *is* dead—she was consumed by Orobo, like the seer told you."

"No," Garrius said, more insistently this time. "She would've died, but my brother saved her. I've proven to myself that it's Priscilla—she knows things only the two of us know. She's right here, in the cell next to mine."

He walked back to the bars to call out to Priscilla—softly!—so she could prepare herself.

"Garrius, listen to me. You're not in a cell. There are no bars. Your castle is in ruins—you're being held in a room in the cellar, where the wine barrels used to be kept. There is nothing stopping you from walking out the open door and leaving, except the spell Vladmin has cast on you. He is in your mind, Garrius. Everything you've experienced and seen since you arrived, it has all been in your mind."

That's impossible, Garrius thought, then said it out loud.

"It requires incredibly powerful magic, but it's not impossible. You and I are speaking right now in the same way. I am reading your thoughts, as Vladmin did, and I am putting thoughts into your mind. Though you hear them as words spoken in person, I am in the forest beyond the castle grounds." There was another pause, then Milos said, "Garrius, you must leave now. I can't do this much longer. The bars aren't real; walk through them and the spell will be broken."

Garrius didn't know what to believe, but he took a few steps back, closed his eyes, and walked forward, putting the cell and its bars out of his mind. He bumped into something solid, though. He opened his eyes; he'd run into a wall made of stone. To his left a staircase stretched upward—moonlight streamed down from above. Behind him, he saw only a short hallway and a large, empty, three-walled cellar. No bars, no cell— and certainly not two cells.

"Quickly," he heard Milos say.

Despite how tired his body felt, and how every joint and muscle protested any quick movements, he took the stairs two at a time and emerged into the kitchen, which had half of a back wall and only a third of a ceiling.

"Go over that half-wall," Milos said. "Take the back way."

"What about Vladmin?" Garrius whispered.

"It's everything I can do to protect you right now. The spell he cast on you is very powerful—I won't be able to contain it much longer, and it will go wake him up. I'll be able to protect you better when you're close."

Milos's voice was so insistent that Garrius obeyed all of his friend's instructions. He leapt over the back wall of the kitchen and ran around the outside of the castle and down the hill, racing his legs despite their protest, propelled forward by Milos's half-encouragement and half-desperation.

At the edge of the forest, he allowed himself to stop and collapse against a tree trunk. Surrounding him were not one but three familiar faces: at the center, his young friend, a strange turban tied around the top of his head, perhaps (Garrius thought) to mask the injury he'd suffered at Garrius's hands; to his right, a young woman whose wide eyes shone with admiration at Garrius in the moonlight, as those same eyes had shone up at him many years before; and to Milos's left, an old man with wrinkled skin and a long gray beard to make up for his hairless head, the healer with whom Garrius had left Milos.

"I know you're tired," Milos said to him, "but we need to put distance between us and Vladmin."

Garrius pushed himself off the tree with an effort of will, and looked around. "Where are your horses?"

Milos smiled, that impish smile that even having a sword plunged into his head didn't seem to have faded. "The wind is our horse," he said.

He reached out for Garrius's hand, as did the young woman, Anya, the princess who had once wanted to adventure with Garrius Arilius and now seemed to be getting her chance. Elder Sakrov held her hand and Milos's, so that together the four of them formed a circle with their arms. Milos turned to the Elder and nodded. Garrius felt energy pulsing through his arms; he was so focused on the sensation—it felt as if his muscles were contracting under a great strain, but the feeling wasn't associated with any pain or discomfort—that he didn't realize what had happened until Milos and Anya let go of his hands and he looked up.

They were in a small chamber lit by candles. Shelves surrounded the room like guards, and were bursting with scrolls and books. A large desk that stretched across the width of the room at the far wall was covered with parchments, scientific apparatus—an abacus, tubes, vials, metal tools of various shapes—and a large tome set on a stand, that appeared to Garrius to be a reference volume.

Before he could ask where they were, the wooden door came open and several men carried in enough stools for all of them. By their long white robes, the same as the one worn by Elder Sakrov, he figured that Milos had transported them to the Dinuvian monastery, though Garrius wasn't sure how wise that was.

"We are in my private study," Elder Sakrov said in his slow, methodical, well-articulated, professorial speech, as if he expected his audience to be taking notes even in private conversation. He sat on one of the stools.

"So I gathered," Garrius said, taking a seat as well. By accident or design, the stools were placed in a circle; they only had to reach out their arms and they could be joined again instantly, and perhaps whisked off somewhere safe if a quick escape were necessary.

"You don't have to worry," Milos said, "we're safe here."

Despite having been rescued from torture and near-certain death at the hands of his brother, Garrius's eyes narrowed as he focused them on Milos. "You're reading my mind still?" he said, in a voice that had caused more than a few of his opponents to abandon a battle before it had even begun.

Milos looked so mortified that the answer was plain.

"I can assure you that he—" Elder Sakrov began,

but Milos was already saying apologetically, "I wouldn't do that, Garrius. I just—your concern was written all over your face."

"I apologize," Garrius said, looking around the circle and conscious that his tone had seriously affected the mood of those who'd risked their lives to save his. "My recent experience has left my nerves frayed—and left me too sensitive." He brought his hands to his forehead and dug his fingers into the skin, as if he could work out the headache that lingered in his mind.

Elder Sakrov studied him for a moment, then rose wearily from his stool and placed his hands on Garrius's head. He drew them away immediately, then seemed to steel his will and replaced them. Garrius felt the pain ebbing away.

The Elder stepped back when he was finished. "The headaches and nausea were caused by your brother's presence in your mind," he said as he sat back down on his stool. "And by his interference in your thoughts. I've never seen anything like it, though. It's a wonder your mind didn't collapse on itself."

"Another couple of days, and I think it would've." Garrius felt more like himself again; felt that his thoughts were clearer than they'd been in almost a month. He looked around at the three again and smiled with genuine relief and gratitude. "My mind thanks you for rescuing it from that fate. But my earlier concern was not for myself—it was for the safety of this monastery. I do not want my presence here to endanger it."

"We are safe," Elder Sakrov said. "For a while at least. We will be able to detect if and when your brother uses his magic to scan these buildings—and we will be able to mask your presence initially, especially if his suspicions aren't aroused and he doesn't probe too deeply."

"Are you sure? My brother has grown very powerful."

"No one knows that better than me," Milos said, "but I have turned my power over to Elder Sakrov, and though I wouldn't say that together we are Vladmin's equals, I believe our power is sufficient to protect you here."

Before Garrius could ask what Milos meant by turning over his power to Elder Sakrov, he saw a spasm seize then release the Elder's face.

"My brother?"

The Elder nodded, sweat having broken out over his bald head. "He has scanned us. The deception has worked, but he will return when he does not find you anywhere else."

Garrius still had a thousand questions, but he pushed them aside and said, "What's our plan?"

The blank stares that met his were not encouraging.

Anya, who hadn't yet said a word in his hearing, broke the silence. "Our plan ended with your rescue. We were hoping you'd tell us how we could help you after that."

She still spoke to him with so much admiration that Garrius felt a strange compulsion to disillusion her, to remind her that he was no longer the man, dauntless and brave and strong, who had been mildly embarrassed by her young girl's crush and hero-worship.

"I don't believe I can defeat my brother," Garrius said. "There was a time when I was strong enough to resist his magic. But I have grown weaker in mind and body, and he has grown stronger." He shrugged. "Milos, you know how powerful he is. Can you withstand him? Can you defeat him?"

In the flickering candlelight, Elder Sakrov's wrinkled face displayed a look of keen displeasure. Before Milos could answer, the Elder said, "I have taken a vow I can never break, not even to stop your brother. I cannot cast a spell to harm a life, let alone to take one."

Garrius knew better than to argue with a Healer of Dinuvia about ethics and necessary evils. Instead, he returned his gaze to Milos.

The young man understood the question in the look Garrius gave him. "We've discovered that I have a lot of power, but it's rather undisciplined," he said. Garrius had never heard someone sound so sheepish when he should've sounded vainglorious and immodest. "I just don't have much of a mind for learning spells others have written, though I'm okay with spells I come up with myself, like the one that saved my life." He tapped a finger against the turban on his head. "But I'm best, it seems, at enhancing the power of others."

"We sensed his energies as soon as he regained a bit of consciousness," Elder Sakrov said. "After that, he helped with his own healing—he was able to channel his power through my mind. That is how he has healed so well in such a short time."

"I don't desire my brother's death," Garrius said. "If there is another way...." He let the thought trail off. "Elder, can you sap him of his power?"

Elder Sakrov shook his head, but it was Milos who responded. "We could kill him, I think, if he were sufficiently distracted and we sent at him everything we had. But to subdue him mentally and try to take away his power? There's no way. It would be like trying to wrestle an elephant off its feet and pin it to the ground."

As Milos spoke, Garrius finally accepted a decision that he knew on a certain level he'd already reached much earlier.

"Then I see only one choice," he said. "You need to send me away. Alone. Then when Vladmin scans this hospital, as deeply as he wants, he won't find me and he won't detect any deception."

"No," Anya said, speaking to Milos. "Wherever we send him, Vladmin will find him. We can travel together, staying one step ahead of Vladmin. I know that there are people who will do anything to protect Garrius—my father is one of them."

"I can't risk endangering anyone else," Garrius said, firmly. "Anyway, there's a place I must go alone, where I believe even Vladmin's magic can't reach me."

"Where?" Milos said.

"Quisin." The word slipped out of his mouth so easily. It was said of the Old Witch that she was like a drug; Garrius knew that the first time he decided to consult her, on what now seemed a minor issue, fully trusting in his own ability to resist her temptations. He promised himself never to return. On his second visit she preyed on his honor and asked him to sacrifice himself—life and soul—to save Milos. He'd unraveled her words and uncovered the solution before it had to come to that. But now he hardly hesitated to return a third time. He'd heard that no one had ever survived a third visit.

Elder Sakrov's lips curled up in disgust at the sound of the name of the Old Witch's town. Her magic was antithetical to his own; his was the business of healing people so they could live a healthy life to a natural old age; hers was the acquisition of souls to increase her powers and extend her own life to an unnatural length. No one knew how *old* the Old Witch was; stories of her had been passed down for centuries.

Milos's look was knowing and Anya's confused. "The seer can protect you?" Milos said.

"Yes," Garrius said, as Elder Sakrov jumped to his feet and, shaking, yelled, "That is enough! You will not speak of her in this place!"

Before the Elder had a chance to clear the confusion on Milos's and Anya's faces at his outburst, Garrius stood as well. "Send me there now," he said, grabbing Milos by the shoulder. "Before Vladmin decides to scan this place again. If he knows you are responsible for saving me, he will kill you, kill Anya, kill everyone here and turn this whole monastery to dust. You have to trust me."

"I can't do it without the Elder," Milos said.

Elder Sakrov was still on his feet and shaking with barely-restrained anger. He seemed to want to cast them all out of his room—perhaps even out of the monastery. "I won't help take you to—that place."

Garrius felt a hand on his arm.

When he looked over at her, Anya started speaking in a soft voice that drained the tension from the room. "When I was a young girl," she said, "the captain of my father's Guard—a man I knew and loved—decided he wanted the throne for himself. He had those men he knew were loyal to him arrest my father, my mother, and myself in the middle of the night, then sent those men to slaughter the guardsmen and army generals he knew were loyal to my father. My father still had some friends, though, and through one of them he was able to send you a note. When he told me to be brave and that salvation was coming, I asked him how many soldiers you had in your army. He laughed and told me that you didn't have an army. I thought my father had lost his mind, for what could a single man do against a High Guard twenty strong or an army now taking orders from the usurper king?

"You snuck past the army and broke into the prison," she continued. "I remember exactly what it felt like when you picked me up in your arms as if I weighed nothing, and carried me out. Then—when we were stopped by the Guard just outside the castle walls—you put me down behind you and patted me on the head. Twenty swords were pointed at you, but you gave them your back and gave me a wink... and I knew there was nothing to be afraid of. You talked half the Guard into laying down their arms rather than continue to rebel against their rightful king. Then, when the captain led the remaining half in an attack against you, you disarmed them all effortlessly. You were a force of nature, a tornado spinning from one person to the next, knocking them back or down, ripping their swords right out of their hands.

"Later you asked my father to reinstate as many guardsmen, from the first half who laid down their arms and from the second half that you disarmed, as would swear to you personally that they would sooner lose their lives than betray their true king ever again."

Anya's hand had been resting on his upper arm. At some point in her story, Garrius had let go of Milos. Anya now faced Garrius with her whole body and squeezed his arms, as if to add emphasis to her words. "You are the bravest, strongest, most honorable man I know. Whatever you think is best, we will trust you and aid you in whatever way we can."

Garrius swallowed hard. Over the years, so many

people had expressed their gratitude to him in so many ways, but none of it had really registered. But now that he felt weak and wasted, it seemed he was finally humble enough that compliments could reach him. He nodded because he didn't trust himself to respond in words, then cleared his throat softly and said, "You need to send me to Quisin. It's the safest place for me." He hoped Milos was true to his word and not reading his mind; otherwise he would realize that Quisin was the very opposite of safe for Garrius. But it was best for them and for everyone that he go there; it was the one place where his presence wouldn't endanger anyone else.

Anya nodded and turned to face Elder Sakrov. "I don't know what your reservations are about Quisin," she said, "but I have heard you speak of the things Garrius has done for your Order. He is now asking you to trust him."

Elder Sakrov stared at her.

Undaunted, she continued, "Elder, send him where he needs to go."

After a few moments, the Elder broke their stare and cast his gaze to the ground. "We'll have to take you there," he said, in a thin voice.

Without wasting any more time, Garrius reached out his arms to the two men. As soon as they took them, he felt the pulse of energy course through his muscles, the strange painless contraction, then felt his feet sink a little in mud as the pungent smell of stale urine rushed into his nostrils.

"You must return," Garrius said to them. "Vladmin likely knows of our history together, Milos. Until you hear from me, you should pretend that you are still healing from your wound. He has no reason to suspect you were behind the rescue—or even that there was a rescue at all."

"I hope you know what you're doing," Milos said, looking around with the same distaste on his face as the first time he'd visited Quisin. "She'll never forgive me—or herself—if it turns out bringing you here was a mistake."

"Go," Garrius said.

The Elder stared with a mixture of fascination and disgust at the wooden door in front of them. He blinked hard, as if breaking a spell, then took both of Milos's hands in his.

"We must leave this place," he said, and they disappeared.

GARRIUS knocked on the door, which swung open. Inside, the severed heads littering the walls stared at him with unblinking eyes, unnaturally wide and frozen smiles spread over their faces.

"Many evil things are spoken of me, Garrius Arilius." He looked around for the Old Witch, but she wasn't in the small room. "And yet didn't I warn you not to return a third time? As I warned these others not to return!"

At their mention, the severed heads seemed to come alive and began to scream or plead with him to free them. Some, he saw, had fresh tears streaming from their eyes.

"Silence!" the old woman said, appearing out of the darkness. She wore the same black cassock that covered her entire body, the hood pulled over her head and cloaking her face in shadow.

"Before you leave here, your soul will belong to me," she said, balancing herself on the skull-topped cane. "Your head will join the others." Her voice suddenly took on a lustful quality that sent chills down his spine. "It will be a pleasure to add your life force to mine, Garrius Arilius. You will share all your secrets with me, and you will serve me forever in the afterlife."

"You sound very sure of yourself," Garrius said. He forced a confidence he didn't feel; it was instinct that brought him here, instinct that made him feel this was the best course of action, even if it meant a third visit. He'd never doubted his instincts before—Thephis had always led them, he'd felt. But then again, he was no longer the man he'd once been; why should he expect his instincts to be as true as ever?

The old woman was cackling and saying, "Yes, I am sure. No one has ever survived a third visit to my humble hut." She let out another short burst of cackles. "I sense your thoughts, Garrius. You think even if you lose your soul to me, your god will save you. But that is the danger of dealing with a seer." She waved her cane at the severed heads hanging from her wall. "Many of these people too have cried out to Thephis. But I would only accept their souls on condition that they bind their god with an unbreakable pledge to not attempt to free them. I have been at this for a very long time."

"Perhaps too long," Garrius said. He couldn't help but look at the faces on the wall and imagine his own among them. Remembering the Elder's revulsion at the mere mention of the town where the Old Witch lived, he also couldn't help but feel that her very existence was an insult to Thephis, who couldn't act without violating the terms of an oath his followers freely made. "Because you just don't want my soul, do you?"

he continued. "You want to win it from me. You want sport; you want me to know I had a chance to defeat you but failed. Go on then, give me my sporting chance."

Help me, Thephis, he prayed. *I haven't made a pledge to her* (*not yet anyway*, he couldn't stop himself from adding). *Help me and help these your servants if there's a way.*

"Ask your questions, then."

"Is my wife alive?"

"She was consumed by Orobo, as I told you already. Orobo was a creature your brother conjured for that express purpose, as I told you already."

"What is his plan now?"

"He doesn't have a plan. He only has hatred."

"Can I stop him?"

"You? No, you don't have the power."

"Milos?"

"Yes."

"Is there any other way to save my brother?"

"Save what? His life? Vladmin will not stop until one of you is dead. Save his soul? After you defeated him, Vladmin withdrew to the distant north. He'd thought himself a powerful wizard, but your mind could resist his spells and your body withstand his attacks. He pushed himself further and further north, into conditions that have killed lesser men. He had to rely on his powers to survive against the elements and against the many enemies he made. He practiced his magic twenty hours in a day, eating and sleeping only enough to keep himself alive. He did nothing except with the goal of strengthening his powers, driven by his hatred of you—and mostly of Priscilla. And in that blind and destructive search for power, he discovered dark corners of the universe and made deals with dark creatures to learn their secrets. There are not enough good deeds in this world to save his soul."

"You're not making a compelling case, old woman. You're telling me that the only way to stop my brother's single-minded campaign against me is to kill him."

"Yes."

"But if I kill him, I am damning his soul. It will fall prey to all the dark forces he called upon during his life."

"No, his soul is damned already. He has damned it himself."

"And if I don't kill him, and he kills me?"

"Like I said, he has no plan, only hatred. Once you are dead, he will find that he is not satisfied, that just as Priscilla's death wasn't enough, your torture wasn't enough, driving you out of your mind as he felt you drove him out of his wasn't enough—and certainly that your death wasn't enough. He will turn his hatred on the rest of the world. He will kill heroes because they remind him of you, destroy villains because people like them opposed you, overthrow kings and turn kingdoms to dust just to prove he can. The world has never seen the likes of the tyrant your brother will become."

"Again," Garrius said, "neither option, my death or Vladmin's, is very appealing to me."

"But it's bigger than you or Vladmin, isn't it?" the old woman said.

The words sent another chill down Garrius's spine. "He's found them?"

"Found them?" The old woman cackled again. "He is trying to kill them. Only Milos's power, funneled through Sakrov's mind, is protecting them. For now. But as soon as Milos's power falters, or Sakrov loses his concentration for even a moment, Vladmin's blast will rip through them and nothing but blood and guts will be left of those who risked their lives to save yours."

"Why? Does he think they're hiding me?"

"No, he knows you're here. He wants them dead because he knows they helped you escape."

"And then?"

"He will come here and demand I release you."

"Will you?"

"Yes. I don't know if my power is enough to resist your brother's, but I am not keen to find out. Besides, he is only interested in your life, whereas I desire your everlasting soul. We can both have what we want."

Garrius looked back at the closed door.

The old woman's snort brought his gaze back to her. "You have no horse. And even if you did, your friends would be dead before you were a third of the way there. Vladmin's concentration does not wane and he hardly feels the effort; the strain on Sakrov is now so great that he cannot possibly recover. He knows that he is dying, and will not survive the night even if he stops struggling now. He is trying, but he will not be able to hold out against Vladmin much longer. I give him another ten minutes at the most."

Rushing forward, Garrius grabbed the old woman, intending to demand an answer from her. Her body felt frail in his hands, like dry twigs. She looked up at him and as the hood fell back a little, enough shadow left her face that he saw her for the first time. Two dark pin-point eyes set in a sea of gray, wrinkled flesh. A small hole where her mouth should have been.

"What are you?" he said, drawing back.

The hood fell back over her face as if on its own. "Old," she said, almost defensively. "But you have more pressing concerns. I revise my estimate—I give Sakrov another five minutes before he collapses. I can send you there in under a second. I can place you behind Vladmin with a sword of pure fire in your hand; you'd just have to drive it through his heart. Or, if you want, I can send you in the path of Vladmin's blast—the sacrifice of your death will cause enough confusion that Milos will be able to escape with Anya. But you should know that the first thing Vladmin will do is chase them down and kill them, so on balance your best option is the first."

"The sacrifice of my death," Garrius repeated. It was as if the words were a key that unlocked a puzzle, a puzzle that resolved into a map; he suddenly saw, as if in a single glimpse, what needed to be done, the only chance he had to save himself, to save his friends, to save the souls of the severed heads hanging on the old woman's wall—and maybe even to save his own brother, life and soul. But would it work? If Thephis willed it, he told himself, it would work.

"Three minutes," the old woman said.

"Send me—not behind Vladmin or in his way. Send me beside him. And no sword of fire or any other weapon."

"Do you know what you're asking for, Garrius Arilius? You are asking for my help. You know the price. Say the words, or leave by that door."

"I pledge my soul to you," Garrius said, quickly. "You will have my life force and my soul will serve you."

"I sense deception in you. What are you thinking?"

"You don't get to read my thoughts until I'm dead, old woman." Then, in a more formal voice, he continued, "Even if I should cry out to him to save my soul a thousand times a thousand times, I ask my lord and god Thephis not to interfere, for my soul is the price I pay you for this service I've requested, and let no man or god of honor rob you of your payment."

No sooner had the last word left his lips but Garrius felt himself pushed from behind. He put out his foot to stop himself from falling, and it touched not the wooden floor of the hut but grassy ground.

In front of him stood his brother, both arms outstretched, waves of fire pouring out of his fingers. The heat was so intense that Garrius had to resist the urge to step back. The noise too was overwhelming, like a roaring river. The target of the flames was a blue sphere enveloping the monastery, solid enough that Garrius couldn't see into it, but not so solid that he didn't notice thin lines forming along its surface. It looked like a large, lined blue egg—one whose shell was about to crack.

Of course they're trying to protect the whole monastery, Garrius thought. Vladmin would've burned the whole thing to rubble, killing everyone inside, if Milos and the Elder tried to escape or to protect only themselves.

"Enough!" he yelled, in a voice that still managed to rise above the roar of the flames. Vladmin turned to look at him, but his arms didn't flinch.

"I'm the one you want, Vladmin. Let these others go."

Vladmin shrugged, and Garrius saw how effortless this was for him. "They stole you from me," his brother said. "They could've stayed in their palace and I never would've bothered them. They could've married and had a thousand little princes and princesses, and I never would've disturbed their peace. But she had to ask about you"—although he wouldn't have thought it possible, it seemed to Garrius that the intensity of the flames increased—"and now they have to suffer for it."

Garrius took a step towards Vladmin, but stopped at a look from his brother. "I'm sorry," he said, speaking softly despite the roar of the flames. "I've never been comfortable around magic. When you started to show powers—I didn't like it. I didn't trust it. It was easier to avoid you than deal with it. You're my little brother, Vladmin, and I failed you. I came here to beg your forgiveness."

"Do you take me for a fool?" Vladmin said, and out of the corner of his eye Garrius saw a second blue sphere emerge from the flames, a smaller sphere the size of a man.

"You want my life," Garrius said quickly. "It's yours."

"You want to die because you wish to be with your precious Priscilla," Vladmin said, distracted enough by the conversation that he didn't yet notice the second blue sphere. "That's why I won't let you die. Suffer, yes, but never—"

"Milos, no!" Garrius yelled, as the smaller sphere split down the middle and his young friend emerged with arms outstretched.

But it was too late. Even as he yelled, Garrius dove by instinct in front of his brother, and absorbed the full force of the blaze of blue fire that had erupted from Milos's hands.

He collapsed to the ground. He heard a yell of anguish—Milos?—heard someone else call for the healers. He felt himself turned over bodily. His insides were burning, the pain threatening to drive him into unconsciousness.

His brother stared down at him.

Garrius tried to speak—it was critical that he explain to Vladmin, crucial that he tell his brother that

Vladmin was wrong and Garrius wouldn't get to be with Priscilla when he died. All was lost unless he could say those words. But his lungs had collapsed and he could barely breathe, let alone speak.

His eyes began to close. The last image Garrius Arilius saw in this world was that of his younger brother, his dark black hair falling around his face, a clear blue sky behind him. His younger brother staring down at him with a mixture of pity and disgust.

HE heard a noise from outside his cell. He saw a small point of light in the darkness beyond. The light grew until it became a sword of white fire, illuminating the fearsome warrior who held it.

The warrior now stood outside his cell. He raised the sword and slashed it across the bars, which disintegrated as soon as they were touched by the flame.

The terrifying figure stepped into his cell.

"Arise, Garrius Arilius."

"I am chained to the wall."

The warrior raised his sword again and swung. Garrius flinched, but the flames were cool to the touch.

"Arise, Garrius Arilius."

He rose. "Who are you?"

The warrior touched the tip of his fiery sword to Garrius's forehead. "I am a man without honor, who has defeated the Old Witch and laid waste to her citadel of death. By the laws of conquest, the souls belonging to her now belong to me."

The Old Witch...death...souls. Garrius returned to full awareness of himself for the first time since he'd awoken in this place. He had died; he remembered now. The Old Witch had taken his soul, as per their arrangement, and locked him up in this prison, a cell much like the one his brother had devised for him. His brother—

"Vladmin?"

"Yes."

"But how did you know?"

"I read your mind, when you were dying. You took a great gamble."

"It paid off."

By the light of the sword, Garrius saw his younger brother smile, a kind of smile he hadn't seen on Vladmin's face since they were children. "Perhaps, perhaps not. But come, there are many souls yet to free. The Old Witch has been collecting for a long time." He raised his sword again and pointed behind him. "Go, Prince Garrius, your princess and your king await. There is a seat for you at his table and a room in his house."

"What about—?"

"Your young friend? He has married the love of his life. I have given them our land; they are rebuilding our father's castle and they will rule over his kingdom."

"And what about you, brother?"

"I am despoiling an old woman whose fear of death made her exploit those weaker than herself, forcing them to sell the only possession of any man or woman that should be beyond price."

"But what about—?"

"Right now, that is all I am doing." One of the flames of Vladmin's sword leapt off and licked Garrius's cheek. "Go on. Your attempt to save my soul has kept you from the woman you love for too long, brother."

Vladmin's sword pointed the way.

Tentatively at first, Garrius walked past his brother. As soon as he crossed the threshold of the cell, the world around him—the fearsome warrior holding the fiery sword and the small cell surrounded by darkness— disappeared and was replaced with another.

Before that happened, though, he heard his brother say from behind him, "You have earned your reward. Be with your wife and rest in your god, Garrius Aril- ius."

About the Author

KARL EL-KOURA was born in Dubai, United Arab Emirates in 1979 and currently lives in Canada's capital city with his beautiful editor-wife. More than sixty of his short stories and articles have been published in magazines since 1998, and in 2012 he independently published his debut novel *Father John VS the Zombies*. Karl holds a second-degree black belt in Okinawan Goju Ryu karate, is an avid commuter-cyclist, and works for the Canadian Federal Public Service.

Karl maintains an online home at www.ootersplace.com, where you can discover more work by him and keep up-to-date with his latest news. He can be reached at karl@ootersplace.com.

ALSO BY THE AUTHOR

Father John VS the Zombies

Civilization has collapsed. The world is dying.

It happened very fast. Within weeks, isolated news reports of people acting in strange and often violent ways became frequent and widespread. Terrifying videos were uploaded to the internet in shocking numbers from across the globe. Chaotic images of societies in rapid decline.

Then—everything went dark. No electricity, no internet, no broadcasts on the emergency radio station.

Now—howling, angry, bloodied creatures claw to get into Johnny Salibi's house, where he lives with his wife and young daughter.

But Johnny and his family are safe. He's boarded up the windows. The door is locked and secure. They will ride things out until the government can get things under control again. They're safe. . .

. . . except that they're not.

Johnny must try to protect his wife and daughter in a world suddenly turned apocalyptic. But things will not go according to plan. Johnny will learn that the zombie plague is not what he or anyone else thought it was. He will learn that the government is not in any position to rescue them. And he will also learn that an unlikely group of survivors might hold the key not only to survival, but to salvation.

Combining elements of zombie fiction, apocalyptic literature, and spiritual thrillers, this is the gripping tale of a man whose faith in God is put to the test with life and death—and even greater—consequences.

Available in paperback and ebook formats. Visit
www.ootersplace.com/FatherJohn for more information.

Ooter's Place and Other Stories of Fear, Faith, and Love

Why doesn't God do something to stop the evil and suffering in the world? Some people who call themselves the "Atheists Against God" think they know the answer. And they know what they're going to do about it, too.

A hired gun—who doesn't use a gun and won't be hired by just anyone—realizes that his profession is killing him, but finds it hard to quit. Until he discovers that his talent has more uses than he ever dreamed possible.

A young boy learns that his best friend is an alien. But does that mean they have to stop being friends?

Meet interesting, complex characters; explore worlds both strange and all-too-familiar; and discover the answer to thought-provoking mysteries in this collection of 13 short stories by Karl El-Koura. Twelve of these short tales were previously published in magazines between 1998 and 2010, while the bonus story is exclusive to this collection.

Spanning a wide range of genres (including science fiction, fantasy, horror, detective fiction, military fiction, and superhero fiction) and a wide range of lengths (from the shortest story at 250 words to the longest at 7500 words), *Ooter's Place and Other Stories of Fear, Faith, and Love* is an eclectic collection. Join the author as he introduces you to stories both light and dark, fun and serious, always entertaining.

Available in paperback and ebook formats. Visit <u>*www.ootersplace.com/OotersPlace*</u> *for more information.*

The Lost Stories:
A Series of Cosmic Adventures

These are the adventures of James Kollins: greedy, petty, selfish captain of the galactic warship *DeVille*; a man obsessed with the holodrama *Captain Courageous and the Women Who Love Him*; a man completely unforgiving of his much-maligned first officer. A man who has just met the Creator of the universe, though he doesn't quite realize it yet, and whose life is about to change in ways he never dreamed possible, though he doesn't quite know it yet.

Find out what happens when an overgrown child in charge of a large military ship, and sadly lacking a conscience and possessed of a strange sense of humor, comes into contact with God Himself, who isn't above playing a few tricks of His own.

You'll be plunged into interstellar war and ultramodern espionage, witness textbook-poor diplomacy and longstanding family feuds, and even encounter a seemingly evil empire of cute babies.

It's a safe bet you'll laugh while reading this book; a virtual lock you'll crack a smile or twenty; and inconceivable that you won't groan and shake your head on a regular basis. In the tradition of Isaac Asimov's pun-in-cheek "feghoots," each of these twelve short-shorts ends in a play on words and phrases that will leave you wondering what's wrong with the author.

Part loving Star Trek ~~parody~~ homage, part spiritual journey, *The Lost Stories* is a series of cosmic and comic adventures that is silly, fun, and also demonstrates the power of God working in the life of even the most self-obsessed warship captain you've ever met.

Available in paperback and ebook formats. Visit <u>www.ootersplace.com/TheLostStories</u> for more information.

www.ingramcontent.com/pod-product-compliance
Lightning Source LLC
Chambersburg PA
CBHW030559130626
46552CB00006B/2602